Mark D'Arbanville is the author of over thirty books of fiction and non-fiction, which have been published in Australia, UK and the USA and translated into sixteen languages. He was born and grew up in London and now lives in Australia. This is Mark D'Arbanville's first contemporary novel. He writes other works of fiction as Colin Falconer.

To the Book Club.

I hope you enjoy

NAKED HUSBAND

with best wishes

Mark d'Arbanville

The
Naked
Husband

Mark D'Arbanville

BANTAM
SYDNEY • AUCKLAND • NEW YORK • LONDON

THE NAKED HUSBAND
A BANTAM BOOK

First published in Australia and New Zealand in 2004 by Bantam

National Library of Australia
Cataloguing-in-Publication Entry

D'Arbanville, Mark.
The naked husband.

ISBN 1 86325 459 5.

1. Husbands – Fiction. 2. Marriage – Fiction.
3. Adultery – Fiction. I. Title.

A823.4

Transworld Publishers,
a division of Random House Australia Pty Ltd
20 Alfred Street, Milsons Point, NSW 2061
http://www.randomhouse.com.au

Random House New Zealand Limited
18 Poland Road, Glenfield, Auckland

Transworld Publishers,
a division of The Random House Group Ltd
61-63 Uxbridge Road, London W5 5SA

Random House Inc
1745 Broadway, New York, New York 10036

Cover and internal design: saso content & design
Typeset by Midland Typesetters, Maryborough, Victoria
Printed and bound by Griffin Press, Netley, South Australia

10 9 8 7 6 5 4 3 2

Acknowledgements

There are agents and there are agents. I owe an enormous debt to my good friend Tim Curnow, I could not imagine offering a book like this for publication if he had not also been my agent. My heartfelt thanks to Jude McGee at Random House, for her encouragement, her support and her vision. Thanks also, at Random House, to Peta Levett, Karen Reid and Zoe Walton. And finally, but not least, to my editor Jo Jarrah, for her wonderful work on this book.

The guiding hand behind this cannot be acknowledged here. But the inspiration given and the courage required to see it in print, I will remember, always.

One

The day Anna died she was driving home from her office in a black BMW and there was a draft treatment on the back seat, a telemovie script on marriage and infidelity. I can picture her now, she perhaps has one hand in the console sorting through her compact discs for just the right song, but she would have felt the presence of that script like a kidnapper sitting behind the driver's seat.

Sometimes I imagine I am there in the car with her, in the passenger seat, as I was so many times. I can smell her perfume, Lancôme Trésor, my right hand is resting on her knee, she is wearing a black top with army green pants, low around her snake hips, a tie at the waist. She is distracted by the traffic on the Fulham Broadway, and frowns as she turns to the right to check for oncoming cars.

But on the day she died she did not check nearly well enough.

Her friend Sally, following two cars behind, saw the

accident. She told me later she did not understand how it happened. Suddenly the BMW lurched forwards onto the road and was struck from the side by, ironically, a removalist's van.

The BMW was slammed onto the footpath, the front passenger side bent around a light pole. Sally found Anna unconscious in the front seat, trapped by the dashboard, which had folded itself over her legs. Her long black hair was already matted with dark blood.

Sally could not understand how it happened but I think I can. I suspect that even as she was looking along the road for traffic, her eyes rested far away, on Paul perhaps, or on me. She was often in two worlds at once, this one and another parallel universe that existed only in her own head, but was probably more important to her than the real one.

The accident was how she had once described it to me, how she had rehearsed it so many times in her head, her car lurching into the path of an oncoming truck, t-barred in a roar of exploding glass and metal. This was her way out.

Anna died a few moments before the ambulance arrived at fourteen minutes past five on a busy Friday night, and that was when our secret affair ended.

Mark D'Arbanville

Two

I am standing in the doorway of the ICU. I recognise her only by the name written in black felt pen on the removable panel above the bed. Her head has been shaved and her face is swollen from oedema, her eyes taped shut with micropore. She is in a medically induced coma. She has been intubated but is breathing unaided at least, though her respirations are so shallow I can barely discern the rise and fall of the sheet. The sound of her heart rhythm on the monitor is an uneasy reminder of mortal fragility.

The paramedics had resuscitated her in the back of the ambulance. She was not breathing when they got her out of her car. A delay of another minute or two and she would have been gone.

She has been in surgery for ten hours, her doctors battling to repair that complex and enigmatic brain. I smiled only once on the five hour drive on the motorway, imagining what the neurosurgeon might have found; I hope he made more sense of the wiring in there than I ever did.

I close my eyes and see again that smile that so often stopped my heart, not as she is now, bloated, pale, and unrecognisable.

There is an intravenous line to her right hand, but the other lies pale and small and limp on the bed, like a wounded bird. She looks so cold. I want to lie beside her and warm her. She always felt the cold so much; *you're always so toasty,* she said. I remember the night in Reims when I let her put her feet on my back to warm them.

She thinks her hands too small, baby hands she calls them. But I adore them. It is these small hands that first took mine in a hotel lobby more than two years ago and somehow took my heart.

They are all gathered around the bed; her mother and father, her brother, her sisters, her husband. They look around at me now, startled. Their faces mirror their confusion and fear. It is her father who speaks first.

– Who the hell are you?

Mark D'Arbanville

Three

Who the hell am I?

It is something I have yet to discover. For the last two years I have been unsure. Before that, I was content to be just, well, comfortably numb.

Soon after I began my affair with Anna, I asked an old mate for his advice.

– You have to remember your home comforts, Greg said, spooning the chocolate off his cappuccino into his mouth, and leaving a brown stain on his upper lip. – Just don't let Sue find out about this.

But this is not about keeping an affair secret from my wife, this is not why I need to talk to someone this cool autumn morning. I feel as if I have run full tilt into a plate glass window. I didn't see this coming.

I first met Anna sixteen years before this, at a film festival. I had joined a group of about a dozen young writers and hopefuls like myself to eat the cheapest pasta dishes in a crowded

Italian restaurant in Notting Hill. I didn't even speak to her, but I still remember the effect she had on me and I still can't explain it.

There were three reasons I didn't speak to her that night: she was with another man; I didn't believe in love at first sight; and I was about to get married in a month's time.

Segue forward a decade and a half to a fancy London hotel and a screenwriting conference; I am not as young, no longer as idealistic, and certainly not as broke. There are a lot of industry people, producers have booked rooms to hear pitches on fifteen minute turnarounds. I see her on the other side of the room, and just like the first time, it is suddenly hard to breathe.

I lose her in the crowd milling around the registration desk, but later I am introduced to her and several other producers by a screenwriter friend. I only have time for a cursory and cool shake of her hand before the next session gets underway.

But I promise myself that this time things will be very different. This time I will see her again, and I will find out what this breathlessness means.

What it means is that my life is about to change, utterly and beyond recognition.

Mark D'Arbanille

Four

My life turns while I am reading the newspaper, bored and distracted, sitting on the balcony floor of the auditorium while below a panel of earnest young writers debate alternative structural narrative in the modern cinema. People drift in and out; bearded men with shoulder bags and power-dressed women with huge red earrings and book bags. Suddenly she is there beside me, touching my arm with her hand, soft, warm and fragrant.

She is the most beautiful woman I have ever seen.

– We are all getting together in the coffee shop, she says. Why don't you come and join us?

My heart hammers in my chest. She is just being friendly, she cannot possibly be interested in me.

I sit for a while gathering myself, don't want to appear too keen. Finally I wander across the lobby, she is with two other indy people but she has her back to me, my heart leaps again, like a kid in class too excited to behave. I join the group, don't talk too much to her, tease her about her professed hangover, try not to be too obvious. Already I like her too much. I am aware of her presence constantly.

I will be for the rest of my life.

Mark D'Arbanville

Five

That night in the lobby bar there is the usual crowd, two other screenwriters, or drunks as they call us in the industry, four thirty-something indy executives, sprawled on leather banquettes in the cavernous atrium. There is the glitter of straw coloured wine, glasses smudged with lip gloss, the slurring of the piano bar crooner.

Anna has a million watt smile that is bestowed equally on everyone so I do not presume it is just for me. She is talking animatedly to one of the other writers and I think I have imagined this connection I feel with her, it is impossible, she is too beautiful for me.

Yet I sense an affinity with her, how she jars with the world, uses her smile as brilliant disguise, as I do. And as others drift off to their rooms she stays, and I stay too. But finally at four o'clock in the morning, we find ourselves alone in the lobby.

The night clerk is dozing at reception.

I am aware of the silence. Is she feeling this same knowing, does she see the same things in my eyes that I see in hers?

– We met once before, I tell her, expecting a frown of confusion.

– The Gallo d'Oro, she says, naming the Italian restaurant in Notting Hill. You were at the other end of the table with a girl with short fair hair.

I was with Susan that night.

So then I ask her the question that is to haunt the next two years of my life.

– Can I ask you a personal question? Do you have . . . you know, hundreds of boyfriends, or just one very lucky one?

– It's complicated, is how she answers, and she picks up my hand in both of hers. I'm married.

Small hands with manicured but unpainted nails, hands that will, over the next two years, reach for mine as we walk along the street, fingers that will coil into my hair as we kiss. The touch of her electrifies me then as it always will.

– Are you happy? I ask her.

– Is anyone?

She rides the elevator with me to my room, where she stands by the window staring at the black, lonely towers of the city. She asks for a glass of water. A message is blinking like an emergency beacon on the bedside phone.

I inhale her perfume as she turns, the sour residue of wine mingles erotically with the strawberry sweetness of her mouth. It is a kiss I will remember for a lifetime. I have never been kissed like this.

I am shocked, like falling into a cold pool on a hot

Mark D'Arbanille

summer's day, life pushing me in the small of the back, but I wanted this or I would not have waited here on the edge. This is not a gentle falling, this is a crash tackle, and I am numbed by the speed of it, my fingers tighten around the rail of this runaway train even as it drags me God knows where. My head is telling me to stop but for once my heart takes over.

As dawn leeches into the sky we take a taxi together to the airport and while I am checking in I finally tell her that I am married, too, and that I have a teenage son. The look on her face scares me, I don't want to lose her, not yet, so then I lie to her and say I am already separated.

As I walk away from her through the departure gate there is a steel band clamped around my chest. I have never felt anything like this before.

The flight passes in a moment. I am dazed and numb. I know I have to see her again, cannot believe we have been thrown together by chance like this, unless this is meant to lead to something better for us both. I don't understand this feeling or where it is taking me.

Even if I had known, I would not, could not, have stopped.

Six

Sue knows there is something wrong when she sees me at the airport. I behave like an actor who has forgotten his lines.

Susan is ash blonde, petite and fearful. The look on my face must have warned her. She receives a cursory welcoming kiss, evasive responses to searching questions.

We hardly talk in the car. I am antsy and distracted.

Home is a rambling two storey house in Hanford, an hour's drive out of Manchester. David is at a friend's. I make coffee and hide in the study, claiming work pressures. Sit down and stare at a computer screen. Jesus.

I don't sleep with her that first night home, tell her I am overtired, that my snoring will keep her awake. What follows is a week of unbearable tension and uncomfortable silence. David picks up on it straight away. He arrives home that afternoon from his friend's place, and immediately shuts himself away in his bedroom.

– What's wrong, Mark? Sue asks me one night, in the kitchen.

– I don't know. I should be happy.

There's water leaking down the kitchen cupboards. Christ. Forgot to turn the tap off. Can't concentrate on anything.

– You've been great to me, Sue, I tell her, thinking aloud.

She touches me lightly on the shoulder.

– Perhaps you need some time to sort yourself out.

– Maybe.

– Why don't you go away on your own for a while. Go to Nepal.

– And do what?

– Find yourself.

Find myself. Like I have been inadvertently mislaid.

I wait for this feeling of dislocation to pass, but it doesn't. I try to get Anna out of my head. I can't.

Every night for a week I work late on the computer, or that's what I tell Sue. Actually I play Solitaire, too distracted to concentrate on anything else. I come to bed after Sue is asleep, so there is no possibility of sex. But I can't put this off for ever.

Finally we are lying side by side in the dark, rigid, like those stone effigies on the tombs of ancient kings and queens in Westminster Abbey.

– What's going on, Mark? she whispers.

– I don't know, I tell her, which is a lie that is also partly true.

My feelings for my wife are confused; they consist mainly of comfortable familiarity and frustration. I have been pacing my comfort zone like a caged tiger for years, watching my time slip away. There is no longer passion, or vulnerability, or much common ground.

But I don't want to hurt anyone. This is apparently my focus now, not hurting anyone.

– If I ask you a direct question, will you give me a straight answer?

I know what is coming and hold my breath.

– Did you meet someone in London?

It takes too long to respond, my hesitation answer in itself. I finally hear myself say yes.

– Did you sleep with her?

I tell her the truth, no, I didn't, but she doesn't believe me.

– Why are you like this if you only talked to her?

Good question. Why am I? I don't really have an answer.

Sue gets out of bed and I hear the bathroom door lock behind her. She runs the shower to muffle the sound of her crying. I lie there in the dark, paralysed with guilt and confusion. This wasn't supposed to happen. I have a perfect life and a perfect marriage.

Just ask anyone.

Mark D'Arbanville

Seven

By then the perfect marriage had been over, though neither of us realised this, for four months.

It had ended at dinner one night, halfway through lasagna and salad. David suddenly announced he wanted to go to boarding school. He is sick of school, the crap teachers, the crap friends, the general crap.

I looked across the table at Sue.

It is the moment we have both thought about for years; we have money, we can travel, we are free. Sue has always wanted to go to Venice.

Dread settles in my gut like cold fat. I realise now why I spend so much time working, so much time away from home; it is because I no longer want to spend time with Sue. It is not a healthy independence, it is avoidance, pure and simple. We invite other couples on holiday because we dread being alone with each other.

What is the point of being together when you don't want

to spend time together anymore? I love her, but in the way of caring, not wanting. Something is irretrievably lost and I do not know what it is, and I have been too frightened to look.

– We'll think about this, I said to David, and in that moment I think I heard the sound of a bathroom door slamming shut four months later.

Mark D'Arbanille

Eight

There are rituals to married life. The most basic ritual is sex.

I segue back in my mind to last year, the rain beating like copper nails on the tin roof. Sue rolls towards me in the darkness and I feel her warm breath on my cheek and her hand strokes my penis and it starts to engorge under her expert ministrations.

I know that tonight it will be too quick, and it is not going to be enough. When did it get this way? When did it start to be sex without desire?

I start to kiss her breasts and then down her body but she pulls my head towards her and tells me she wants me inside her now and it is too soon for me.

She knows my body well. It is obedient. I know what she wants but even as I climax there will be a part of me that is disappointed.

I come thinking of someone else, lonely inside my own

head. She rolls me onto my back and I kiss her breasts and tease her nipples with a saliva-wet thumb, and she comes, silently gripping the headboard, as she always does.

Afterwards we both lie there engaged in our own thoughts. We have absolutely nothing to say to each other because there is nothing in what we have just done that we have shared.

But we are together. I have been mostly loyal. She has been a good wife. There is consolation in not living alone.

Except that I am.

And so is she.

Mark D'Arbanville

Nine

They say women can fake an orgasm, but men can fake a whole relationship.

Every woman knows of course that all men think about is sex. Sue told me once that this is how I achieve intimacy and that I know no other way.

If this is true my attempts at intimacy elsewhere were still-born. There was a one night stand in Frankfurt that left me racked with guilt, and a young student who fell in love with me at one of my screenwriting classes and did not care that I was married and had a family. When I told a squash partner about it, he laughed and said not to worry because oral sex wasn't adultery. I was flattered by her attention but ended it almost as soon as it had begun because what I really wanted then was my wife back.

I took my wedding ring off four years ago, complained it was too tight. By then I could tell myself absolutely anything and I would believe it.

We sleep back to back and have done for a long time. I wake each morning to the hard arch of her spine, the inter-twining of arms and legs now surrendered to a solitary foetal gathering from the marriage. I sometimes spoon in to her in the mornings but there is not the intimacy I crave, these are habits of physical intimacy only. There are parts of her cordoned off, roadblocks in her soul, we are warring cities under siege. There is truce for sex and for society, but among the darker streets of her soul I am not welcome.

Occasionally I look at the wedding photograph on the wall. Christ. We were both so young.

Back then I knew what was going to happen. I was going to be a writer, I was going to travel and have the perfect family and live in a big house away from the North London terrace where I grew up. At the time I was living in a cramped inner city flat and the only writing I had ever sold was a sitcom that never went past a single pilot episode, never aired.

We were broke.

But I was determined to realise my perfect life, the promises I had made to myself like pictures cut from a glossy magazine.

Sixteen years slipped past too fast, the last few frittered away like coins in a penny arcade, suddenly my pockets are half empty and I wonder where my bank has gone.

But I have achieved almost everything I set out to do. My life is almost perfect and I cannot understand why I cannot force the pieces to fit the puzzle, bang these square pegs into my ideal round holes.

And a voice inside keeps nagging at me: if this is the almost perfect life, how is it I am always imagining another one?

Mark D'Arbanille

I tell myself I will be happy one day, when Sue and I have sorted things. Meanwhile David needs help with his homework, there is work, her work, friends to see, dinner parties, birthday parties, and it is only when everyone has gone home and we must we sit down and search for things to say to each other that I realise this is not enough.

I feel like a fraud. It has been an award winning performance, being a man who is loved and successful. I have fooled everyone except myself. I feel like one of those cheap spaghetti western sets, a whole town made out of plywood, but if you walk through the door of the saloon or the barber shop, there isn't a damn thing on the other side save a view of the desert.

A year and a half before I meet Anna we have our fifteenth wedding anniversary and we book four days at a resort in Antigua.

When we arrive, a hurricane has wrecked the gardens, there is a sense of desolation, everything slashed back. Our bungalow looks forlorn without the crush of foliage around it. There is a swarming of dragonflies, an anomaly of the storm, hanging in metallic clouds over the dimpled green surface of the swimming pool.

Sue and I make plans in the sun loungers in the languid heat of the afternoon; she wants to see Venice, learn another language. It is the last time she expresses a desire to do anything other than get through a day. It is the final blossoming of our marriage though I do not know it then, a sudden winter blooming that will fade in the passage of a few nights, like desert flowers.

Later we lie in the bath in our bungalow and she plays with

my penis with her toes. It is a long time since she has been playful like this. I start to make love to her and crack my head on the hot water tap and we both laugh. We go into the bedroom without towelling off, leaving puddles on the polished mahogany boards and soaking the bedsheets.

That night we celebrate our anniversary in the restaurant, the surf drumming on the reef. We eat honey prawns and drink champagne. Her eyes dance in the candlelight, the first time in years they have not been clouded by doubt.

Everything is perfect; it reminds me eerily of an awards night. It is time to receive the plaudits, this is everything I wanted. I have climbed my mountain. What is this nudging that there should be more? Is my heart half full or half empty?

Somehow I feel as if I have plagiarised my own life.

She looks away for a moment and I see the doubt and sorrow return to her eyes. When she catches me looking her smile reappears suddenly, as if she was hooking up her bra strap, a moment's forgetfulness.

Her buoyant mood evaporates as we are leaving next day and when the aircraft touches down in Manchester the stranger is back.

A week later as we lie in bed I ask her where the Antigua woman has gone.

– The reality is, you can't have that all the time, Mark. It was a holiday. What do you expect?

– Are our lives really that bad? We have a fine son, we can travel whenever we want, we have good friends. What more do you want?

– You're being unrealistic.

Mark D'Arbanville

Unrealistic. We fight, again, finding new ways to say the same things; I want more, and she can't understand why I can't just let things be.

Fighting gives us both the illusion that we are doing something. It is our way of relating. If we stop fighting we will have to risk, move on, and we are both terrified of that.

It all ends in tears, as it often does, for this is what our marriage has become for me; the fight that one day I will win, one day I will persuade her to be what I want and everything will be sorted.

I feel cruel and guilty and shabby; cruel for hurting a good and decent woman, guilty for wanting more, and shabby for making another compromise I know will not satisfy either of us, a compromise that will eat up another few weeks or months and nothing will change.

I feel keenly the time passing, both our lives frittered away on these sordid battles. I want to laugh and have fun again. I want to feel connected.

Instead I just feel scared and confused and trapped.

Ten

Almost a year passes, nothing changes, and I somehow convince myself that things are better. But in reality something must be desperately wrong, even work does not seem to matter to me anymore. But I tell no one. I will fix this myself. I am too proud to tell even my closest friends that my life is slowly derailing.

At least Sue and I have stopped fighting.

One Sunday afternoon I take her for coffee. We lean in, a man in a tweed jacket at the next table rustles the *Sunday Telegraph*, muted Wynton Marsalis floats over the chatter and the hiss of the Barista coffee machine.

I am going to sort out my life and hers over skim lattes.

We both agree we are not connecting. From now on, we say, we will get together at least three times a week for coffee, go to dinner. I lean back, pleased with how things have gone. I have fixed everything, it's what I do.

– The only solid thing in my life right now is our relation-

Mark D'Arbanville

ship, I tell her, thinking this is what she wants to hear. It is what I want to hear.

She doesn't say anything. I know what her enigmatic smile means and she is right. It's not perfect, but I tell myself it's better than it was.

– I've booked to go to lunch tomorrow, I tell her.

A frown.

– For Valentine's Day?

A difficult silence.

– I'm working that day, she says. We have an important meeting at the office.

I stare at her, bewildered.

– Can't you get out of it?

– The partners are all going to be there. I can't just drop everything for you.

She slams her cup down on the table. She will brook no more argument.

– What time's the meeting?

– Twelve thirty.

– Well, when will it finish?

– I don't know.

– Who the fuck arranged a lunchtime meeting on Valentine's Day?

A shrug. Right. She did.

In truth, she frightens me. Her face can get so cold, so shut down.

– At least I remembered.

– You want me to stand up and applaud?

– Most husbands round here don't give a fuck.

– We ignore each other every other day of the year and on Valentine's Day I'm supposed to be grateful?

– Gratitude? Heaven forbid.

A cheap shot. My first port of call when I'm bruised.

– The reality is, Mark, you just want to pretend everything's all right when it's not.

She is probably right, and I don't like it.

– If I live to be a hundred I'll never understand women, I hiss at her. It's an exit line and I leave, stage left. Dramatic, plus I have the last word. Why don't I feel good about this?

That afternoon when David gets home from school, he hovers. Sue is in the kitchen chopping vegetables for a stir-fry. I am on the phone to my writing partner, she is telling me about a screenwriters conference coming up in London later in the year.

– Are you doing anything tomorrow? David asks Sue.

A loaded question. Why is he asking? I wonder if he's noticed something. I look at Sue, my ear to the phone, waiting to see how she will answer.

– We don't have to go out for Valentine's Day because the media says so, Sue tells him.

The look in his eyes. Fear.

– You always go out on Valentine's Day.

– If we don't do anything any other time, Sue says, why make Valentine's Day an exception?

I turn to David and shrug my shoulders. Your mother, the look says.

That night we go to a friend's birthday party. Sue stands in a corner, talking to Greg's wife Trish, not drinking, looking bored, as she always does.

Mark D'Arbanville

– I think I'll go home, she says at eleven o'clock.

She has had one drink. I have been drinking light beer all night, thinking I would drive and that for once she might give in, let herself go, have a good time. The last time she let her hair down was over a year ago, we had a weekend away with three other couples at a resort hotel and she got drunk in the spa and I had to carry her back to our room. She was giggling but sobered up fast and that evening at dinner she was sour and irritable, angry at herself for losing control.

– I just did it to please you, she tells me later.

I want to dance, drink, have fun. Is this too much to ask of your wife, for Christ's sake?

So tonight, once again, I give her the car keys and she goes home on her own.

– I'll see you in the morning, she says.

At two o'clock I get a lift home with friends.

Next morning when I get up, she is in the kitchen, making tea and toast. The distance between us is crushing.

– How was last night? she asks.

– It was okay.

Silence. That's it.

I put cereal in a bowl. She is wearing a white terry towelling dressing gown. It's like she is wearing a polar bear.

– Do you want a cup of coffee? she asks me.

She puts the kettle on and walks out of the kitchen to the laundry. This is not a marriage. I don't know how to fix this, don't know that I want to anymore.

– I don't think I can do this anymore, I tell her when she comes back.

A silence that goes on for ever.

Finally:

– Are you leaving?

– I don't know.

The look on her face: Christ, I can't hurt her this way. But what am I going to do?

Mark D'Arbanville

Eleven

That night I find her crying alone in the bedroom. I hate myself for causing this so I hold her and tell her everything is going to be all right. After she is asleep I lie there staring at the cold dark, feeling weak and angry because this is not what I wanted, it's just another postponement.

I feel trapped in this life and cheated of what I want from this marriage, sex and love and passion and intimacy and fun.

I start to get angry again. Why do other people pack their bags and leave and I still wait, looking for an excuse?

How long do I keep trying to fix something long after I've stopped really wanting it fixed? Isn't it enough that I am desperately unhappy? Is it because I have not told my friends and family, I can't make this dilemma real for myself?

I am too private, too secret, a victim of the perfect world I have created. I am always saving other people, listening to their problems, doling out advice, but I won't ever admit my misery to myself or anyone else.

Our marriage is a carousel without ponies or lights or music. It just goes round and around in frustrated silence. I am too scared to step off, there is no better reason that that. Round and round and around, going nowhere.

Mark D'Arbanville

Twelve

Spring passes to summer and summer to autumn. A bad relationship, a bad marriage, picks your pocket of seasons, of whole years, can even steal your whole life. It is now just a week before I am due to fly out for the screenwriters conference in London.

Sue is sitting in bed, hunched over her book in a baggy white T-shirt. She has a stoop to her shoulders these last years, life is too heavy, there have been too many fights, every cigarette does you damage, every fight leeches a little more from your soul. Rain lashes the window like a rash of small stones. I hate our bedroom and I never want to sleep in here again.

She tosses her book aside.

– What is it, Mark?

I sit down on the edge of the bed and try to tell her what it is, but somehow I can't put my frustration into words. Whatever I say will sound either stupid or mean.

– I just want things to be more like they were, I hear myself telling her.

– Not that again.

The greatest unhappiness in my life is reduced to not that again. I know she is going to destroy my arguments with her cold logic, and it won't make any difference because I'll still feel the same.

– The reality is, you want us to be like we were when we were nineteen. It can't be like that, Mark.

– Why not?

– Because people grow up.

– I haven't.

– Obviously.

Nice one. Walked right into that. Score ten points for Susan, the opposition takes an early lead. I close the bedroom door so David will not hear another fight.

Sue thinks this is about sex. I think this is about sex.

– Shall we see someone?

– See someone?

– A marriage counsellor.

I have been afraid she will suggest this. We went to a marriage counsellor once before. He gave us rules for better communication. But I don't want my love affair reduced to rules; how she asks for more help with housework, how I ask for oral sex.

I don't want to communicate with Sue better; I want to feel alive again, feel connected. My heart has silted over, the workings rusted up. I worry that a counsellor will send us back to try again at the marriage like naughty schoolchildren, with a lecture on sharing.

Mark D'Arbanille

The worst of it is, I know what Sue wants from me, I don't need a marriage counsellor to tell me that. I know I do not love her as I could, that I am holding back so much. The problem for me now is that even if I knew how to do it, I wouldn't want to. And the guilt over that has turned me dead inside.

– What do you want me to do? she asks.

– Play foozball with me, I tell her. Foozball is what David and I call the arcade table soccer game now gathering dust in the back shed.

– Is that what this is about? Foozball?

– No, it's not about foozball.

– Then what is this about?

I am spoiling for a fight is what it is about. I am tortured by feelings of restlessness and entrapment. So I drag up some minor incident of the past to bitch about. Another few minutes and we are both screaming at each other, scars many years old opened up again and bleeding.

She shouts at me that I am shallow and self obsessed. I tell her, at the top of my lungs, that she is self righteous and rigid. A part of me stands back and watches in horrified fascination this wellspring of anger, this man I do not recognise, a man I do not like and do not want in my life anymore.

Now David bursts into the room, *stop it, stop it,* and he and his mother are both staring at me, I am to blame, of course.

I get in the car and drive and drive. I stop the car an hour later and look around, wondering where the fuck I am. There are lights in a farmhouse at the end of a dark driveway, the blue flicker of a television screen, other lives quietly and peacefully underway.

Christ. How did things ever come to this?

The worst of it is, no one will ever know what happened tonight. I won't mention this fight to even my closest friends.

The reality is – as Sue loves to say – that I feel cheated of the love I need and it is turning me into a monster.

Sue and I are like two heavyweights battering each other to a standstill, never a winner or loser, we rest for a week, perhaps two, until the bruises and cuts have healed sufficiently and we are both strong enough to go another round.

I drive home. The house is dark, Sue has gone to sleep in the spare room. My worst fear now is that David will find out how dire things have become between us. This is my focus now, keeping the truth from others.

Why is it so important to be so fucking perfect?

I fall asleep alone in the cold wastes of the double bed but in the morning Sue and I are both awake and dressed before David gets up so he will not know we have slept apart. She is dressed already, a grey pants-suit, smart, businesslike, white rollneck jumper under her jacket.

We are civil to each other at breakfast because we are just too exhausted to fight any more.

– What are we going to do, Mark?

– We'll talk tonight, I tell her without looking up from my coffee.

But we don't talk that night because David needs a lift to school for a drama rehearsal and we are both drained from the fight the night before so we watch some television and go to sleep.

By the time we talk again it's a week later and we spend all that time pretending there is nothing wrong.

Mark D'Arbanville

Leaving still seems unthinkable. We have rusted into each other's lives. I cannot let go of the lumpen certainty that she will always be there, someone to take to friends' parties and family gatherings.

I tell myself I am trapped when I am just too scared to walk away.

A week later I kiss Sue goodbye at the airport and go to a writers conference in another city and run full tilt into that glass wall.

Thirteen

Two weeks after the conference I find a reason to go back to London, work of course, a script conference with a producer at Channel Four, but the real reason is that it is where Anna lives, and I tell Sue I am going to see her. I still won't say the words that need to be said. I seem to think an affair will revitalise my marriage and make it better. I think I will learn something from Anna that I can bring back to my marriage and it will make me a better man.

The problem is, I have always thought that every marriage was retrievable, and I feel that unless Sue agrees it is over, it is my duty to stay in it and make it work, whether I want to or not.

I have only just begun to realise how much of my life, my values, are tangled up in a thick underbrush of guilt and obligation. How did love ever survive?

The answer, of course, is that it didn't.

Stripped back to ugly, it is this: half of me is still not sure

Mark D'Arbanville

that my marriage is over, even though another part of me knows that it patently is. So I put myself in the position where Sue will end it for me. I cannot deny, even to myself, that this is gutless but I am also genuinely confused. I always thought that if I ever left my marriage, it would be because I did not love and care about my wife.

And I don't want to dismantle this perfect life I spent fifteen years creating. I don't want to lose control.

I wait for Anna in the lobby of my London hotel. She is smiling but tension betrays itself in her small bird-like movements. I cannot believe she has come. We walk to a pub on Gloucester Road.

The sun is yellow bright this autumn afternoon. We pass families with pushers, businessmen talking on cell phones, extras in this the first act of our story; to them we are perhaps just two business colleagues on our way to a meeting.

We sit on bar stools, by the frosted window. Anna has on a pink scarf, her hair tied back with a tortoiseshell clip.

– You're beautiful, I murmur, almost in awe, the first time I have ever allowed myself this transparency with any woman.

I witness a look of disbelief and gratitude on her face, as if no one has ever said this to her. A well-fed skinny girl and she is starving inside.

– When I met you, at the conference, I didn't know you were married, she says.

– Would you have waited up for me if you'd known?

– You've got a son. I don't want to break up your family, anyone's family.

– My marriage is over anyway, I say, and I know it's true but it's the first time I've heard myself say the words, even to myself. I have not, even at this late stage, told anyone that our marriage is in such desperate trouble, not my friends, not my family. I cannot believe I am saying these things to Anna. It has never been this easy before to tell someone how I feel.

– Have you talked to her, Mark?

– It's all we ever do. Round and round in circles. We've just grown so far apart. I have tried. I have really tried. I am lonely and miserable. I just want it to end.

She takes my hand, holds it gently in hers. She is married, too. This is all wrong. I don't care.

– What about Susan?

– She's happy with things as they are. I'm the one with the problem.

– Perhaps if you talked to her. You could work things out.

I shake my head.

– I hate feeling guilty that I don't love her more. I don't even want to write anymore and it's all I've ever wanted to do. If I can't write, what am I going to do?

She astonishes me by kissing me gently on the forehead. I breathe in the scent of her from the valley swell of her breasts. Warmth, sex and refuge here, sweetly offered. I take it.

I take her arm and my lips touch the warm and velvety skin inside her elbow, feel the soft pulsing of blood. This new

Mark D'Arbanville

man is frightening, he follows his heart blindly. Who is he and why is he trying to take over my life?

I carry her to the bed. We kiss for hours, there is no rush, and I know anyway that this will end too soon. Finally, we start to make love. She claws at my face, as if she is trying to push me away, even as she pulls me closer, her eyes screwed shut as if she is far away and in pain. I sense there is something here I do not understand. She throws her head back on the pillow, such narrow hips, I am as gentle as I can be.

If only I had remembered that caution in the next two years, had been as gentle outside the bedroom as I was in it.

Fourteen

The next morning Sue rings. It is a rehearsed speech.

– I said you could take whatever time you wanted to sort out what's been worrying you. I thought that was a gift because you might make choices not in my favour. I thought you would go somewhere neutral.

Somewhere neutral would have been pointless. I had to discover if my feelings for Anna were illusory. I wasn't going to discover that on a mountain in Nepal. But she is right, we should have separated when I drove away that night, should have said the words.

– You chose London, where she is, you took advantage of my trust and generosity of spirit.

That seems a little off the mark to Mark. But I let that one go.

– For my integrity and sense of honour I am withdrawing from the relationship. You need to find somewhere else to live when you get home.

I mumble something back. Fair enough, probably. I have set it up that she has thrown me out, instead of walking away first.

I always despised myself for that.

Fifteen

The grey slick of the Thames slides beneath us as we drive over Westminster Bridge. I look out of the passenger window at the commercial towers cramping the grey dome of St Paul's, the postcard view of the parliament buildings. I am crossing my own divide, I do not know where this will take me and I know there is no way back.

As she drives Anna talks about her life. I recognise someone very much like myself, trying to orchestrate a perfect life, like posing a family photograph, but someone always makes a face or blinks at the wrong moment.

– Do you love Paul?

– He's all I've ever known, she answers. We've been together since I was 21.

She looks at me as if she has told me a lie and wonders if I will call her on it. It is true, she has been with Paul for ever. The lie, I suspect, is that she still loves him. Or perhaps, that love is what she really wants.

Mark D'Arbanville

– What about before you met Paul?

– When I was sixteen, there was this guy, he was an actor. Michael. He always had a string of girls following him around.

– Did you sleep with him?

Her face takes on a petulance.

– That's one thing I'm grateful for. I never slept with him. He never loved me.

The hurt is still naked in her voice. It sounds as if no man has ever really treated her decently. I tell myself I will somehow be different.

– He loved me seeing him with other women. Jealousy kills you. I promised myself I'd never be jealous of anyone again.

We stop for dinner at a small village in Oxfordshire. She wants to book into a room over the pub. Instead we sit on a wooden bench by a mill pond and I ask her to drive me back to London, leave me at the hotel, go home. Guilt has me by the throat.

– What's the point of that? You're here now. We have today, we have tonight. Can't we have that? What difference will it make if you go back now?

I can't answer her, can't explain this overpowering sense of foreboding.

– I don't know if I can do this.

She gets out of the car and stamps across the cobbled square to the pub. A few minutes later I get out of the car and follow her inside. She is signing a credit card slip at the bar for a double room.

– I'm not taking you back to London, she says over her shoulder. That's crazy.

I take the bag upstairs and while she showers I debate with my conscience, by the window, staring down at an ancient horse trough and a red telephone box.

When she emerges it is twilight and the room is soft lit with bedside lamps. She is wearing one of my grey woollen jumpers that reaches almost to her knees. She melts my heart.

Later, as she kneels over me, stroking the hairs on my chest with her fingers, I hear myself tell her that I love her. It is the only time in my life I have heard these words come out of my mouth unbidden and unexpected. We both stare at each other in shock.

My God. She has touched something in me that I did not even know was there.

Sixteen

It is only one weekend and it is gone too soon. We drive back to the city to Paddington station. This is the first of many last times there will be for us. We huddle together behind a news kiosk in case we are seen together. I hate the bladerunner crowding of the terminal, the garbled echo of the tannoy jangles my nerves.

Very soon I will come to despise train stations and airports.

As we wait, I listen to her describe a barren sex life with Paul, how remote he is. She tells me he never sends her flowers, shows her no affection in public. I cannot imagine how such a perfect woman could ever be taken for granted this way.

– All I wanted, once, was to find a way to make him love me, she says.

Her huge blue eyes take on a faraway look. She can conjure her own pain faster than anyone I have ever known.

– I remember going to his parents' house once and sitting

on the front step, crying. His dad came down to try and comfort me, in the end.

She screws a wet tissue in her fist.

– He had an affair once. I put all his things in a suitcase and put them outside the door. Then I brought them in again. I did that five times before he came home. I knew I'd make him love me in the end.

I try not to think too hard about this, about this woman I have fallen so utterly for treated with such disregard and disrespect.

– When did it change, Anna?

– I don't know that it has.

My train is about to leave. We stand up and walk towards the platform. We pass luckier lovers hurrying hip to hip towards the exits. Our story is the grimmer one, tears on stony faces.

As my parting benediction, I tell her to leave him, as if it is up to me to tell her how to fix her life.

I hold her face in my hands and kiss her one last time, hoping to keep this image of her in my mind, as sustenance for the lonely years ahead when I dream of her. I have no intention of starting an affair.

I say goodbye for the first time, thinking I will never see her again.

Mark D'Arbanille

Seventeen

Three hours later I am sitting in a chrome and plastic diner in Manchester talking to Sue on my cell phone. I tell her I will have the rest of my life to regret what I've done. At the time I think this is true.

She is implacable.

After I hang up the phone I get a text from Anna: *Missing you already.*

I think what I have done is unforgivable, as if I have blown up a building. I call Greg and tell him I need a bed for a few days, that Sue has kicked me out, and why. He already knows what has happened and says Trish has made up the spare room.

Hanford is an old cotton mill town now gentrified by new money, Beemers parked in the narrow country lanes. For years I have enjoyed being part of such a small and close-knit community; now it feels like living in a goldfish bowl.

I don't want anyone else to know about this, want to work

this out with Sue in a dignified way, between ourselves. But in her rage and distress she has told everyone in the village what a shit I am, asked my friends to talk some sense into me, let me know how much pain I have caused and get me to come home. She works at a large accountancy firm, might as well work at a radio station.

The marriage was apparently fine until I ran out on my responsibilities for a bit of skirt.

Is this what it is?

I am trapped by my own need for privacy. Everyone supposes I have done this on a whim, that it is mid-life crisis, sex, insanity.

I try to ring David from Greg and Trish's. He won't come to the phone.

I am surprised to find that I don't back down. Anna has shown me there is life after the falling out of love. Every time I think of her there is this stalling of the heart and I wonder if she feels the same way.

Yet I still feel obligated to take this lesson in loving back to my own marriage eventually. I do not want to hurt my wife.

I write Sue a letter: *It was never my intention to leave our marriage. But I had to get my head sorted. I know you cannot possibly understand, but the only place I could do that was in London. I want to somehow rediscover what we once had. My only hope is that you make no irrevocable decision about us, that you leave the door open.*

I won't let go, because I am not just giving up a relationship, I am giving up friends, a way of life, the whole perfect

Mark D'Arbanille

picture. There are dreams I have cherished for a lifetime, an apartment in London for weekends, more time to travel.

But life doesn't give a damn about my perfect picture. Instead it wants me to change myself and the patterns that have dogged me for a lifetime. It wants me to be a part of my own life.

It wants me to risk.

And among the lies and hesitation and confusion, I know there will be no lasting resolution to this until I do.

Eighteen

I remember creeping into David's bedroom when he was eighteen months old.

He is asleep, his thumb in his mouth. I listen to the gentle rhythm of his breathing in the dark. I take one of his fingers through the bars of the cot and hold it, gently. I feel a tear tracking down my cheek.

I cannot leave him. I cannot miss watching him grow up. I have to try again.

The memory of this is so fresh.

Where did all that time go?

Nineteen

The thing that Anna loved about me, that made her feel safe, was that I was not looking to use her, I did not want just a quick affair. She was right about that. But it was this very thing that left me without defences in the end.

I am in my study and there is a text on my cell phone.

How did you get into my heart so fast? I can feel your constant presence.

Later that week she calls to say she is flying to Manchester on business, arranging finance for a feature film with big money from Dublin. Perhaps we can have one last time together? I know I have to see her.

U have swept me off my feet and made my heart soar so high I can hardly breathe. I love you.

In that moment I fall for her completely. How could I not? How could any man not fall in love with a woman who writes this to him?

Right or wrong, for once my heart is leading the way, scything ahead, into dark and unknown places.

Another text from Anna: *Remember I am a liar, cheat and I can hurt you.*

Fire, then ice. She is trying to warn me, telling me there are things here I might not understand. I text back: *OK so you lie, cheat and you are going to break my heart – nobody's perfect.*

I think I'm being funny and clever. But even if I had understood what Anna was trying to say, I don't suppose now it would have changed a damned thing.

Mark D'Arbanville

Twenty

It was Sue's kindness that bound us together: she painted my study when I was away on a fishing trip; there were cups of coffee brought to my desk, chocolate bars that appeared beside the keyboard, subscriptions to sports magazines that arrived unheralded in the mail.

I tried to return her consideration with lover's gifts, but the roses delivered to her workplace embarrassed her, and she asked me not to send them again. Her responses left me bewildered.

Is kindness enough? Should I live out the rest of my days with comfort and familiarity and the security of knowing she needs me, and never have the temerity to ask for more?

Knowing, too, that I can give so much more?

These are velvet ropes and I am softly bound.

Twenty-one

-**A week since I got back** from London. We choose a meeting in neutral territory, like two warring dictators. Hanford, the little village where I live, is alive with gossip. We have brightened many people's lives with this, something to talk about in the pub, for the wives to dissect at book club.

Sue, in her terrible hurt and bitter rage, maintains an intolerable pressure, telling me it is over, while telling friends I am a bastard but she wants me back. I make only rare efforts to explain myself. I can't explain myself. I don't really understand what has happened and anyway, I feel I deserve it. Guilt has left me paralysed.

We sit in the cafeteria at the municipal swimming pool, winter drawing in outside, depression sinking into the bones like ink into chalk. Sue is pale, her face tight as a mask. Her latte is cold and she pushes it away.

She is dressed down, as she often is, a black track top, black shapeless cords. No make-up. Like a chameleon she always

Mark D'Arbanville

endeavours to blend into her background, her smile painful and perfect disguise.

My mind drifts back ten years, this same indoor swimming pool. David is still small, just four years old, achingly funny and precocious. We are playing crocodiles. I lie there with just my eyes above the dimpling water in the toddler's pool, arms akimbo like crocodile jaws. I splash after him and he screams and tries to get away.

I stand up and look at Sue, sitting in the café reading a paperback.

– What about getting changed and coming in?

She smiles and shakes her head.

David splashes me and runs off, shrieking with delight at his own bravado. Sue returns her attention to her book.

Almost ten years on and just a civil word is progress.

– **What are we going to do, Mark?**

– Do? I thought it was over.

– The reality is, Mark, you want to have your cake and eat it too.

– That's not reality, Sue, it's just your opinion.

I wish I had not muddied the waters with another relationship, but until I met Anna I didn't know there might be something else for me, something better. I thought Sue was right all these years: this is just the way it is.

I think about how long we've been together. We can't throw that all away.

Can you measure the worth of a relationship in years,

I wonder? Never mind the quality, see how far back we go? What is love, a relationship? Is it a safety net, a habit, something that once you have committed to, you endure, no matter what? Just an insurance policy against being alone?

I wonder how many other couples live out this same desperate compromise.

– Every marriage has its ups and downs, Sue says.

I imagine David's face when I tell him that his mum and I are divorcing. I think about selling the house and who gets what and who goes where and what Sue will do. I think of the vacations and the hard times when I was starting out, about the friends who will not understand and how everything will change.

As if these are all good reasons to stay together.

– What is it, Mark? Do you want someone younger, is that it?

– I knew that was coming.

– Has she taught you some new tricks in bed?

I finish my coffee, look away. What am I going to say to her? She wants me back, and I don't want to go back, but I can't bear to see her hurt like this.

– Let's not do this anymore, but the look on her face at this rejection is like a bullet in the guts.

I try and imagine what it would be like to be happy again, to be fully in love, drinking life up in deep draughts. To feel a bond that is more than the past. To love home more than you love being somewhere else.

– I am sorry it has come to this, Sue.

She ignores this gambit.

– What happened in London, Mark?

Mark D'Arbanville

– I'm not telling you, I answer. I see the relationship with Anna as sacred now and I will not parade it in front of her for her disapproval.

– Are you still in contact with her?

I don't answer and she stares at me, astonished.

– I don't believe it.

When I was a kid my parents told me lying was wrong but they did it all the time, it's how families keep together. What you don't know can't hurt you, my mother used to say. To be a good person you had to keep the people you loved from any painful truth, as if honesty was a luxury to be indulged in sparingly, like oysters or caviar.

Sue says the marriage is over but I know I can still hurt her with this. It is an impossible position.

And once you start lying you can never stop. By protecting Sue from pain, I am quickly turning myself into someone I do not like at all. Sue has assumed the affair is over and I have let her believe it. I am too guilt-stricken to leave the marriage for good but I want another few days with Anna. I am essentially living in an emotional limbo.

I feel pressured by my own contradictions. I thought Sue would never forgive me if she ever caught me out in an affair; but she has. I am shocked. So I leave doors swinging open everywhere, need time to work this out, and time is what I don't have.

– Anna's flying here on business. I'm going to meet her.

– I thought it was over between you.

– Well, it's not.

She gets up and walks out.

Twenty-two

I rent a house ten minutes drive from Hanford, towards the city. It smells of dust, it has been empty for months, cold and mildewed. I leave many rooms unexplored. Like my soul. Spiders lurk in dark corners, shifting uncomfortably under the scrutiny of a torch.

I prowl the creaking house like a ghost by day, surf the TV channels at night as I lie sleepless on the sofa.

Early one morning two days later, Sue's car screeches into the driveway.

– This marriage is over, she screams.

I had thought that for her it already was.

– I'm going to tell David tonight, she shouts, and I want you to be there.

I am not ready for this. My head is spinning. I just want to see Anna one last time, and then I will be ready to disassemble my former life, if that's what is about to happen.

– And if I don't come to the family execution?

– I'm going to tell him my side and if you're not there, that's your problem.

I know already that I won't go. It is my act of rebellion, because I don't know my side yet. Do your worst, I deserve it.

– The reality is, you've got a new relationship, Mark.

– I know you won't believe this, but I don't think Anna wants me as a husband.

– Fuck off, Mark, today is the present, Saturday is the future and you are spending it with her. That's the reality. I deserve someone much better, someone with more honesty, more integrity, and more spine than you.

I agree but that makes her angrier.

– The reality is, Mark, I'm the only one in this marriage with any integrity.

Everything with Sue is about honesty and integrity. Well, I have lived all my life pretending to have honesty and integrity but since I've never really been honest with myself you could say this is virgin territory.

I still love Sue in some way and this is confusing.

– Give me time to think, I shout, but she gets in her car and drives away, her door swinging open as she reverses too fast. The open door hits me on the shoulder and knocks me flat on my back.

A door left open nearly does me in. Even then the irony is not lost on me.

Her last words, shouted through the driver's window, are: *Fuck off, you spineless cowardly lying dishonest asshole.*

Fair enough.

I get slowly to my feet, rubbing my bruised shoulder.

My new neighbour is pruning her roses. I smile and wish her a good morning.

She says good morning back and carries on with her pruning. By afternoon this will be all over town.

Mark D'Arbanille

Twenty-three

She has found an excuse to come north. She tells Paul she has gone to Edinburgh, to another film festival. I meet her just outside Oldham, at a sprawling hotel that looks like a manor house, an hour's drive away.

We almost tear each other's clothes off as soon as we are alone.

Afterwards she watches me in the bathroom mirror, puzzled by my interest. She is on her toes as she applies her make-up. I admire the long curve of her spine, black lace underwear, curious after so long, something uncurling inside me and stretching in the sun again, like after a long hibernation. We have made love all morning and I still have this overpowering desire to run my tongue along the soft, downy skin at the nape of her neck, inhale her.

Sue always shuts the bathroom door.

I love the way Anna wears her clothes for herself, not for me or for her husband, her sensuality is the whole point of it.

Women are still mysterious to me after a lifetime, the perfume, the underwear, the camisole tops, the little jars and tweezers and pink razors.

Sue never likes me to see her naked, and never looks at me unless we are making love. We are never comfortable talking about sex, never ask each other what we like, what we think about in bed.

Sometimes I lay a hand on Sue's thigh as we make love, it slides gently between her legs, the feel of her is magic, thrilling, before she pushes it away. I can be inside her but I cannot touch her. It is a metaphor for what our marriage has become.

— I've only had three lovers, Anna whispers.

She sees the look of disbelief on my face. A woman as beautiful as this?

— I've been with Paul all my life. There was one affair, after he left me once.

— Not before Paul?

— Men were never interested. I used to go to clubs and men would never talk to me. I remember once a man called me an ice queen.

The hurt on her face is disguised as contempt. Like all ice queens she has a heart of glass.

— There was this one boy, he was American. He took me up to his hotel room. I told him I wouldn't sleep with him, so he went down on me. Afterwards he gave me some champagne from the minibar, and we talked for hours. I didn't even touch him.

— Did you ever see him again?

Mark D'Arbanville

– He wrote once. From New York.

New York, a safe distance. The Ice Queen, burning up, but only on the inside, where no one can see. Somehow she has preserved the mystery of her sexuality without losing it to disappointment and fumbling and bleakness.

– I always thought I was better at sex on my own until I met you. I never understood what all the fuss was about.

– I bet you say that to all the boys, I say, trying to deflect this gambit, making light of it.

But her eyes have an intensity of their own.

– No, she murmurs. You make me see love in colour.

No one has ever said that to me, and I had never imagined that any woman ever would. I would die for a woman who said such things.

But she is going to send me away.

I am lost.

Twenty-four

I prowl the hallway outside our hotel room, talking softly into my cell phone. Moth-eaten deer-heads stare at me in bewilderment. There is a smell of mould from the carpets. No one calls me in the rental, but now I have come here with Anna, I am fielding calls from my brother and my friends, worried because they have just had messages from Susan saying that I am missing.

Later, in the spa in our room, Anna's eyes are hooded, her lips wet, her toes stroke my penis under the water.

– Will you leave Paul and come and live with me?

It is as if I have raised some long-held resentment about her mother. She reaches for her drink and looks at me over the rim of her glass with angry impatience.

– Can't we just have this moment?

– Can't we have years of them?

– I told you, I don't want to talk about the future. I can't deal with this right now.

Mark D'Arbanville

That night Anna twitches and jerks in her sleep. I suspect there is something more than the affair that is troubling her. There is a darkness to her and about her I cannot hope to understand.

But the next morning Anna whispers over breakfast, in the cavernous dining room with its chintz curtains and rose-patterned crockery.

– Stay in London with me, at the apartment. Paul's gone to visit his parents in Scotland. You are going to need someone to help you get through this.

– I can't. I have to go back and sort things out at home. What happens when Paul gets back?

She is sulky. Anna lives in the moment, or so it seems. When Paul gets back, will she live in the moment then, too?

The next night I put her on a plane back to London. We sit in my car in the multi-storey car park, as desolate a place for goodbyes as there could be. There is the deafening roar of a jet engine as another flight lifts from the tarmac, tail lights winking, into the cold black sky.

– I wish you were my wife, I whisper.

– I wish I was too.

I wish now that I had got on that flight with her, followed my heart, all the way, stayed with her in London. But Anna was still married to Paul and we both found it convenient to forget that.

Twenty-five

I drive home in the early hours of the morning, the smell of her still on my skin. The headlights pick out the clawing fingers of the trees, and I wonder if this is all a dream. She will not talk about Paul or families or the future, I cannot bear to think what will happen, what is ahead.

I have made up my mind now that I will go back for the sake of David and my wife's sanity. But Sue has changed the locks on the house. Later that day, when she sees the car pull up in the driveway, she runs inside and locks the front door. I call to her to let me in and she hides in a back room.

Everything has been dragged out of the study and piled in the carport. She has torn up some of my old scripts, the early ones, spools of videotape lie around where she has smashed them on the concrete. Is this what love comes to in the end?

I drive out of town and park the car near the old stables. I walk blindly in the rain, soaked through, mind raging. When I finally stop walking, I have no idea where I am. There

Mark D'Arbanville

is a an old mare sheltering under a petrified beech, a portrait of dumb misery. I raise my fist and punch the wooden stile, smashing my knuckles. I watch fascinated as the blood drips off my fingers into the mud.

I imagine my little town wagging its fingers at me now. I am about to lose not just a wife, but a life.

Well then, fuck them. It is my life. I built it. I can take it down.

Twenty-six

I stare at the screen on my laptop. Blank. I have not been able to write a word since this began. My life has been hijacked, not by Anna, but by a monster lurking inside my own skin.

My cell phone rings. It is Anna. My breath catches in my chest every time I hear her voice on the telephone.

She is lighter and freer than at any time I will remember in the next two years; Paul is away and she sounds buoyant. She says that men have disempowered her all her life. I do not want to join this rank of bullies, but I will.

She tells me that I am her best friend.

– Your husband should be your best friend, I say.

She is defensive:

– A lot of my friends have men they talk to. If we were together, wouldn't you want me to talk to other men?

– I mean the one you tell your secrets to. Someone to truly be your lover and best friend.

But she describes a life of compartments, work is front and centre. Her husband is quarantined from her best friend, Sally, and there are other boxes for her parents, for her sisters, and finally her own feelings, which seem to be kept secret from all the other boxes.

Perhaps she thinks our affair will keep her and Paul together. This way she gets to have her life and still have the intimacy that is missing. I know it has been lacking in mine.

All my friends tell me that Sue still loves me. She wants me, so I am obliged to love her back.

Isn't that what love is?

Twenty-seven

An expensive rooftop bar far above Marble Arch, glittering with Moet flutes, Arab businessmen smiling like wolves, gold bracelets flashing in electric candlelight. Snow drifts from a black sky and settles on the glass. I watch the silent passage of tail lights in Park Lane far below. A crooner plays Elton John on the piano.

I hear myself saying to Anna all those things my own wife has longed for me to say, that I have only said until now under duress, morsels of love grudgingly prised from a sticky heart.

The reason I can open up to Anna and not my wife is not clear; I like a rational explanation for everything, and when it is not apparent I invent one. Only a man who has experienced that same breathlessness with a particular woman might understand both my certainty and my confusion; for others it will sound merely fanciful.

She starts to talk again about Paul.

— I love that you open car doors for me, she says. Paul

would never think of doing that, or holding my coat for me. I can be at a party all night and he never checks to see if I have a drink. We both work all day, but I'm the one that always cooks tea.

It is unfathomable to me that she has endured this neglect for so long. To me, she is everything a man could ever want.

– Listen to me, she says. What a whiner.

– It isn't whining.

Why should a woman apologise for wanting to be treated as something to be valued? Why this constant guilt over what she needs and craves?

– Sometimes I don't think we have anything in common anymore, Anna says.

– Then why do you stay with him?

I think because of what she says that she is tired of him and wants to leave.

– He's all I've ever known, she says.

– That's not a reason. Leave him, Anna.

A wan smile.

– Sometimes I see lovers in the street and how much in love they are and I wonder why I can't be like them. You have shown me what real love can be like.

– You can change this, I say.

She sips her drink and looks away.

– I made love to you more in a few weekends than in a whole year with him.

– You deserve so much more.

I feel safe in this role, as her mentor, the one who has been there and knows his way around a failed relationship. Like an actor in a long-running play, I can speak any line for any character on cue and without thinking.

– My whole family think I'm perfect, she says. I'd like to be a little wicked, just once. I'm sick of being everyone's angel.

– I like you wicked.

There is a beat when we look at each other. Her eyes are liquid.

– Well, mister, she whispers, what are we going to do?

She has opened the possibility of talking about the future. But just then the waitress leans in to ask if we want more champagne and Anna's question is left unanswered.

The pianist calls us over at the end of the set, asks if we are on our honeymoon, the way we look at each other, he says, it's like there's no one else in the room.

For me it is like there is no one else in London. Next day, under the lowering skies of Camden Town, we buy mulled wines and wander through the techno fashion stores in the old factory tunnels, all brown brick and punks and Middle Eastern wide boys with East London accents.

In the afternoon we make love in my room as a cold wind buffets the glazed windows.

– Do I exhaust you? she whispers, and gives me that crazy smile, putting her head adorably to one side.

She says she cannot imagine ever not talking to me, hopes we will always be in some way connected. She is writing the last lines before we have even finished the first chapter.

Another man would have made it an affair and nothing else. Another man would have been more ruthless, more cynical.

The naked husband falls in love.

Mark D'Arbanville

Twenty-eight

We are standing in the Tate Gallery, she is staring at a portrait by Rubens and I am staring at her. She is not classically beautiful, the lines of her chin are not perfectly defined and she has an endearing bump to her nose. She has a feminine poise and allure that comes from inside, it is unique and sets her aglow and makes her one of the most beautiful women I have ever seen.

This exquisite woman.

I still have a Kodachrome of the moment here in my mind, though I have tried many times to erase it. Beautiful woman with blue eyes, in black overcoat and pink scarf. By Rubens. A masterpiece.

Surreal present with dark shadows looming. By Dali.

The lover as abstract impression. Picasso.

She has nudged her way into my heart, subversive and soft. My heart is thawing under the heat of her, though she thinks herself utterly forgettable.

She turns and sees me staring.

– What?

– Nothing, I say, and smile.

A moment to carry with me into the future, when she is not there for me to admire, when she has gone back to Paul.

Mark D'Arbanille

Twenty-nine

The elegance of a faded London boutique hotel off Kensington Road. International flags hanging limp on a cold winter morning, buses rumbling past on Earl's Court Road, grey liveried porters with cockney accents and an Australian at reception talking about surfing at Burleigh Heads.

Another stolen afternoon. We burrow under thick coverlets, December frosting the windowpane. I am inside her, hardly moving, I cannot be closer in any way at this moment, inside her eyes, her body, and the moment goes on for ever, I never want it to end.

I have touched the watermark in her soul. I read her body like braille, unpeel her layer by layer, heart dipping and racing.

– Don't ever hate me, she whispers.

I am bewildered. Why would she say such a thing? Why would I ever hate her? What does she mean?

– Just whatever happens. Don't ever hate me.

I have no idea what she means. My naive heart cannot believe she will throw this away.

Thirty

I am three years old and my mother is playing with me on the floor of the living room. I push one of the toys away, an old teddy bear, the stuffing is coming out of its head, and I don't want to play with it anymore.

She picks it up and holds the toy as if it is a small child.

– Ah poor Ted. Don't you love him anymore? He'll cry.

And she makes a crying noise.

I experience a sickening feeling inside. It is the first time I remember feeling guilty about something. I take Ted back into the game.

Rescue. Responsibility.

I have just learned my first lesson in love.

Mark D'Arbanville

Thirty-one

When I was in London I sat in my hotel room staring at my laptop in confusion and despair. I was flooded with emails from Sue.

When I get back to Manchester she will not even answer my phone calls.

Finally we meet, away from the village and the scrutiny of our friends and neighbours, in a steak house in the city centre. We both try once again to resolve what is wrong between us but spend most of the time staring at the salad bar. It is the same conversation we have had a hundred times before, the same frustration.

Like Anna I keep my marriage's meltdown concealed from the scrutiny of my own family. I don't call my brother or my parents for weeks, friends are fed scraps. Sue is talking to everyone, relaying the list of my iniquities, carefully indexed. Me, I am still in denial.

I don't know how to fix this, so I pretend it's not happening.

I want to love Sue, it is the right thing to do, but I cannot make myself. I hate myself for letting her down, for not feeling as I should. But I cannot force myself to go a certain way, my heart has dug in its heels, straining against the obligations I want to impose.

After the fruitless conversation in the steak house Sue again does not answer my calls and will not let me come to the house, so I talk to David on the phone, but he sounds distant, bruised and frightened. He never asks about the separation. His grades have dropped from straight As to Cs.

I wonder if love has anything to do with this. I love my son, I love my brother. Is love the right word to describe what happens between a man and a woman, this mysterious alchemy of sex and that first electric arcing of minds and spirits?

When did this marriage degrade to these demands of need and duty?

It is clear that Sue and I have grown apart; now I must choose between the callings in my own heart and soul and the wracking of guilt.

I so long for more.

But for now I must twist in the wind, riven through with cold spikes of guilt. It is just a fucking marriage. Let it go. But somehow it became a matter of life and death and I don't know how or when that happened.

There is an email from Anna: *I have been unfair to everyone and selfish. I am not single. I cannot do this anymore . . .*

A few days later she calls from Aberdeen where she has gone to join Paul and his family for Christmas. Down the

Mark D'Arbanille

echoing line I wait for her to tell me that she loves him, that the fires are rekindled, that this is really what she wanted all along. I wait for her to say there is no longer a place in her life for me.

But she doesn't.

So I don't let her go. If I had, there would not have been Paris and Champagne, New York and San Francisco, there would be no story, my heart would not have been broken, and I would have stayed the same.

Thirty-two

I have known Jen a long time, we have written scripts together, she has had three marriages – so far, as she says. She has absolute clarity about my situation.

– She just wants a bit of a fling before motherhood. You look like a good fuck. Are you?

We are in the snug in our local, the Wheatsheaf. We both retreat here at the end of a long day's writing. It was a decent pub once, before the chain took over and installed poker machines, a mounted television tuned to Fox Sports and sanitised pub food. Now it's like every other pub in every satellite suburb in England.

Jen has a vodka and a slice of pecan pie from the kitchen, her favourite.

– She wanted someone to make her feel special and beautiful, Jen says. She fills up at your servo, and then goes home to hubby. It's obvious. I bet her friends have affairs and serial sex, and she wanted a dirty little secret of her own. You're such

Mark D'Arbanville

a romantic, Mark. A babe in the woods. It's adorable. I didn't think there were any men like you left.

She spoons cream into her face from the top of the pie.

She chuckles.

— We've all done it, Mark. Seen what it's like with another man. Trouble is, it's like having a cigarette behind the school sheds when you're a kid. You get the taste, suddenly you find yourself buying a pack every week, then you've lost all your pocket money.

Is that it? Was Anna just looking for excitement, for danger, for spice? To get Paul to pay her more attention? If that's what it was, it has worked.

— Like every thirty-five year old woman doesn't deserve decent sex. We tell ourselves it's not important, try to be good girls, when what we crave is a man who'll make us wet, send us flowers and go down on us once in a little while. But then we think we're a slut for wanting that over being dutiful and good.

She is enjoying this, the bitch.

— So now he'll lift his game, right? He'll pay her attention now he knows he has competition. And she'll go for it.

Jen shrugs.

— It's her life, Mark. Not yours. She's been with him thirteen years. It's a lot to throw away. Does her family know about you?

— It won't last, I hiss at her, angry now, feeling shabby about my own resentments. As soon as he feels safe again, it will go back to the way it was.

— That's not your problem. You can't see the future, so

don't try and tell her what to do. Besides, she's a woman. It's her choice. You've been married for fifteen years. What would you know about women?

Another low chuckle. Educating Markie. What a hoot.

But Paul doesn't love her the way I do, I think. But because I love her so much, he gets a second chance. Tell me the justice in that.

I can't stand this. Something sacred has been broken. Like finding a pornographic magazine in the presbytery, a syringe behind the altar. But Jen is wrong about Anna.

I finish my pint of bitter – an apt choice – and leave.

Mark D'Arbanville

Thirty-three

Her work, mine, perfect cover for an affair. She works from an office in Chelsea, always travelling on business, meeting financiers, writers, directors. She talks to me every working day on the phone, never weekends. Her secret life is carefully quarantined. She enjoys the flirting, the phone sex. I think this is natural to her, yet other times she hints that this is somehow out of character. She tells me that when her sister Cathy lost her virginity she never told Anna, because she thought Anna would disapprove. Her family, even Paul, call her their angel.

I cannot imagine this side of her.

But I sense in her an assurance that when the time comes she will do what is necessary to keep her two worlds apart. She knows what is coming. This is my initiation and she bleeds for me, knowing how much this will hurt.

– It's not you, it's me, she says when I ask her again why she doesn't leave him.

– What do you mean?

She does not answer, perhaps cannot answer.

– Your marriage was in trouble for years. You expect me just to do this straight away. I can't do this to your timetable.

– It's your apartment, Anna.

– Where will he go? Could you do that to Susan?

– I didn't have to, she did it to me.

– I didn't ask you to leave Susan. I didn't want any of this.

– I love you.

– I didn't ask you to love me.

– You told me you don't feel any passion for him. You're not happy. You said he bores you, that you don't have anything in common. Why do you live with a man you don't love?

– I do love him, she says, and it is like a shock of cold water.

– Then what do you want with me?

A long silence on the phone.

– He is no good for you.

– I know you only want what's best for me. Thank you for loving me so much. I am really blessed to have a friend like you.

It sounds right, but the words are cold and removed. She is like a small and wounded animal retreating to its cave.

Mark D'Arbanville

Thirty-four

Another business trip, another few days together. It is my birthday; she gives me a cigar case engraved: *To my lover and best friend.*

A chill mist clings to the birches, a hideaway cottage in Duxton, a tiny village in Lincolnshire. The cottage belongs to Jen and Terry and Jen has given me the keys for the weekend. The fire is lit in the grate. We slow dance, there is gooseflesh on her skin, her body curved into me.

Red wine glasses and clothes are scattered on the floor. Candles burned down, wax on the floorboards, a smudge of oil on the sheets. The morning sun splits the thunderheads, like God's finger dipped in a rippling pool, a curtain of rain chasing the sun.

We map the new worlds of each other's bodies; I have discovered the sensitive place in the fold of her elbow; the long, pale neck; the silky skin of her inner thigh.

There is this sense of childlike wonder at what her body can do, and what she can elicit from me.

I know her so well already, when to move fast and when to move slow, and she is a diligent teacher. She grabs my head and pushes my face hungrily between her legs. She sits up, squeezing my hands, screaming in release at her moment, from the private ministrations she has taught.

She likes it when I raise myself above her, to look down and see me inside her, look into my eyes as I come. It is not my own pleasure that thrills me here, just watching her leaves me breathless, the arch of her back, her fingers curled in my hair as she comes.

When we go out she likes to tease me as I drive the car, or we stand in a quiet corner of a country pub and she surreptitiously squeezes her bottom into me and makes me hard and then moves away grinning, saying, *What are you doing? Everyone's looking at us.*

I sense this is a different Anna from the one her family or even her friends ever see, that this is a part of herself she keeps hidden from them all.

On Sunday morning, as I am packing the car, she asks me to come back with her to London. Paul is away again, some family wedding in Scotland, and she has cried off and let him go alone, work pressures her excuse. Driving down the motorway, she undergoes a transformation. She does not want me to talk about the future and I do not want to break this spell, not yet.

Anna says suddenly: *I want you to meet my sister*. So Cathy does know about us, I think, so she must also know what shape Anna's marriage is in. Cathy is two years older.

Anna rings on the hands-free. Cathy lives an hour away,

outside Colchester. When Cathy answers the phone, there is a forced gaiety in Anna's voice, a need in it.

Her sister sounds severe on the speakerphone, not the same laughter there.

– Mark is with me, Anna says. I thought perhaps you'd like to meet him.

A beat.

– We're only about an hour away in the car.

A frowning, I can almost hear it, see the crease in this unseen sister's lips.

– I'm supposed to be going out to lunch, Cathy says.

Anna presses her.

– What about later this afternoon?

Cathy makes some excuse and my life with Anna, in the real world, is stillborn. Anna hangs up, smiles, I smile back, then stare out of the window, at the bleak skeletons of elms, the brown frosted fields.

The smile on Anna's face disguises whatever she really feels at her sister's rejection of her choices. Cathy is being loyal to Paul, but I wonder if her loyalty should not be first to her sister.

Looking back, it seems to me now that this was when the deception really began and our lives divided. They all say they want her to be happy. But what they really want is for her not to make waves in this most delicate of families.

So I never did meet her sister, and I never knew how Anna felt about that. She never said and for once I never asked.

Thirty-five

Women I slept with.

The one who stayed up talking to my best friend in the living room and when he fell asleep on the sofa she crept into my bedroom and the first I knew of her feelings for me was when she put my penis in her mouth while I was asleep.

The one who smoked too much and fucked like an animal but I left her because her mouth tasted like an ashtray. Not one of my finer moments.

The one who made love to me in the front seat of my first car and ended up breaking my heart.

The one who had two nipples on one breast.

The one who screamed and woke up the landlord, and I heard him say through the window: *I think he's murdering her in there*, and when he knocked on the door I told him she'd bumped her toe on the bedpost.

The older woman who gave me her body gently and sweetly and then went home to the other side of the country, and I only realised years later that I wished I had followed her.

The one who made noises like a cat and made faces like a baby and who distracted me so completely I lost my erection every time.

And the one who is best of all. The one who lets me watch her come without me touching her. The one who whispers to me her most secret fantasies. The one who drips melted chocolate on me while I am tied to the bed, the one who looks deep into my eyes when I come inside her like she is looking into my soul, the one who said that I made her see love in colour.

The one who just wants an affair and has stolen my heart utterly.

Thirty-six

We are in bed when the phone rings. Don't answer, I murmur.

But Anna leaps out of bed. Midnight. Something may be wrong, she says, a family emergency.

When I walk into the living room she is sitting on the floor, her bare spine curled against the cold wall. She is naked, the phone cradled in her shoulder, her face stricken.

– Give me the phone, I mouth at her.

She turns away.

It's Sue, I know it.

I discover later that Sue has gone through the emails on my computer, found Anna's name and got her number from the London directory. It is like a brick through the window.

Why don't I take the phone? Stop this now, you said the marriage was over! Instead I let Anna listen to my wife plead her case, and I have never forgiven myself for this, permitting the lie that I wasn't with Anna that night.

Mark D'Arbanille

So instead I listen to my lover talking to my wife. She pours out her heart to Anna but she will not talk to me. It is the worst thing I have ever done. Guilt has turned me into a craven monster.

Why do I do this? Why do I still keep this affair hidden from my wife? Because I have always believed that if someone loves you, you have to love them back and protect them from hurt, no matter that you don't want to, or how trapped and suffocated it makes you feel.

Meanwhile, my wife tells Anna, as she has told everyone, that Anna has wrecked a marriage filled with fun and passion. This assertion is so outrageous it takes my breath away. It is fun and passion that I have missed. She must still think that Anna, who wants me to go back to my wife, is responsible for me being here.

When Anna puts down the phone, ashen and trembling, I know it is over.

— You have to go back to her, Mark.

— My marriage is over, Anna.

— What about David?

— You can't stay together for your kids, no matter what age they are. It's done him no favours, believe me.

But even as I say this, I sense that she always expected me to go back anyway, and she would go back to Paul, no longer vulnerable, in control. Now is the time.

— I can't go back.

— That's your decision. It's your life.

But I sense that she wants me to go back, to absolve her of guilt. This has gone too far for her.

But I can't go back, not after the phone call. I can never forgive Susan for that. Is that what I need, some solid excuse not to forgive, to justify what I know I will finally do anyway?

But because I cannot forgive myself for hurting Susan after all these years, I will let this all turn to crap, I know I deserve it. This is what you get for not making up your mind.

Mark D'Arbanville

Thirty-seven

It is clear that Anna will not leave Paul. I will have to make my own arrangements, without her.

Jen, as always, is eager to tell me some home truths.

– You're angry with her because you wanted to leave Sue and have somewhere to go to. That's why men and women have affairs, Mark, so we can have our cake and eat it too. For a man who's knocked around so much, you really are an innocent abroad.

– I love her.

– It'll pass, she says with such confidence I want to push her face in her pecan pie. Anyway, you haven't really left Sue yet, she goes on, remorseless. Trouble with you, you want Anna to commit, then you'll leave. You want it all set up first.

She's right, of course. I would like the easier option. But she's wrong if she thinks I won't do this, one way or the other. I'm stalling for time before plunging into this icy pool, but I know what I'm going to do in the end, with or without Anna.

– What about David?

– David doesn't talk. David never talks.

– He's a teenager.

– That's one reason, sure.

– What about Sue?

– Oh, she talks all the time. But not to me.

– I'm worried about her.

– Yes. So am I.

– Are you going to see this Anna again?

I nod. I have arranged to see her again in London in a few weeks.

– This is going to fuck you up, Mark. Be careful.

– Talking of fucked up, how's Terry?

Terry is Jen's husband, a solicitor with a six figure salary and an arrogance to match. Treats her like shit, in my opinion. Like the other two before him. But some women don't seem to mind that, it's respect and admiration they can't handle. I realise now that Sue has had precious little of that from me in recent years.

– Think he's having an affair, she murmurs.

For God's sake. In the end, I suppose, we all get the relationships we deserve.

Thirty-eight

The affair has been going on now for six months. Anna no longer calls me. One weekend, on impulse, I drive down to London.

Even in the midst of her greatest turmoil, she looks as if she just got married or won a lottery. You have to know her well to see behind the disguise. One moment she is laughing, then suddenly darkness pours out of her, a thunderburst from a clear sky. So I should have been prepared.

We have been drinking in the Lamb and Flag and afterwards we stagger back to my hotel and make love on the bed. The sex has a desperate edge. We both know this cannot go on. We fall off the bed, I hit my head on the bedside table and split the skin above the eyebrow. There is blood everywhere.

Afterwards I put her in a cab, and she goes to meet Paul at a friend's party. The next morning she rings early and says she has to see me. She picks me up in her car and we stop the car, and as I stare at the Sunday morning walkers with their dogs and small children she tells me she can't see me anymore. She has to get sorted.

I am bewildered. My inexperienced heart is caught in the searchlights.

– You said you loved me.

– Perhaps I just don't love you enough.

– Then tell me you love him.

She won't. She can't.

– What are you going to do? I ask.

– I don't know.

– Why don't I give you the keys to the cottage in Duxton? I shout at her in rage and utter frustration. If you love him so much why don't you take him there, do with him the things you did with me!

She is crying too and beats her fist on the steering wheel in frustration.

– It's not like that!

– I don't understand this!

I imagine Jen sitting in the back seat, smirking.

– Did you do this just to get back at him?

It is Jen prompting me now. Perhaps my devil's advocate had a point. I want to understand what this is all about. But she doesn't answer.

– You have to go back to Susan. She loves you.

– For God's sake, Anna.

– I can't break up your family.

– You didn't break it up. This is my call.

She doesn't believe me. She thinks every marriage, every

Mark D'Arbanville

relationship, is inviolate, even though we have been miserable for years.

– You need someone who can give you what you deserve, Mark.

– This is it for me, I hiss at her between gritted teeth. I'll never love anyone like this again.

– Because I hurt you, you're never going to love anyone again? Is that what you're saying? If that's true, I wish we'd never met.

I stare at her, red-eyed, an agony of the heart. She is killing our affair before either of us will ever know what it might become.

– It's what you did, after your actor friend. Why can't I?

She blanches at the mention of him, the one who broke her heart, made her feel like a fool.

– You love me too much, Mark.

– For fuck's sake, I mutter. I open the door, close it again, agitated to the point of losing control. The irony. Anna, I love too much; Sue, I did not love enough. What the fuck do I do? Is there loving just right, like the Three Bears and the porridge?

None of this makes any sense, and I have always been a man that who needs to understand, wants a logical answer for everything and won't let anything be. An emotional bully.

I just want to hear her say, from her heart: *I really love Paul. It was a mistake being with you. Everything I said was untrue.* Then I can forgive her, and I can walk away because there is no way back.

But she doesn't.

– Fuck this, I say, and get out of the car.

Not the most eloquent or gracious of goodbyes. Not *Casablanca*. She hugs me one last time, pale and shaking, and hands me a card in an envelope. I kiss her roughly and push her away.

I walk blindly, hands in my coat pockets, the cold April wind biting to the bone. It is not the cold that makes me numb. I wonder which is the real Anna, the one who made love to me last night or this other woman who has just told me that she does not love me enough.

I open the letter, take out the card she has written.

*Look after yourself, Mark, you are and always will
be in my heart and I will talk to you every day, you
are the most special man in the world to me.*

Shouldn't Paul be the most special man in the world? Paul is the one she lives with. What, then, is Paul? The most special man in the world gets the rejection and the despair: what does Paul get?

I cannot imagine living with a woman if I thought some other woman was the most special woman in the world.

I tear up the card and watch the wind scatter the pieces across the grass. It has to be a lie.

Mark D'Arbanville

Thirty-nine

Guilt like a sandbag sitting on my chest. Guilt and loss. There is a truck on the road, I see the headlights in the distance. I blink hard against the thought of what I am tempted to do. A blur, like flicking through the pages of a book, certain words jump out and then are gone.

Revenge.

Oblivion.

Release.

Atonement.

For God's sake.

I wonder how much protection the airbag will provide on impact at this speed. I wonder what the truck driver will make of this.

The wheels wander over the white line, I hear the truck's klaxon and the headlights flicker urgently.

The moment of impact.

I feel the draught as the truck rushes past. Some instinct

has brought me back to the right side of the road. What in God's name was I doing? My heart hammers against my ribs like a football. Roads have crossed in my life. The other path finds me crushed and mutilated in a wreck of twisted metal at this very moment.

Life and death. A blurred line on a dark road. A fork in the way of a much longer journey. An instant's decision.

Mark D'Arbanville

Forty

Sue has said she wants to see me when I get back to Hanford. She sounds desperate on the phone. I wonder where such desperation might take her. It would be my fault if she hurt herself, of course. I could stop this.

It is late but she has left the front door unlocked. There is a light under her bedroom door. She calls to me as I walk in, and I am so desolate I reach for her in the dark and cold.

– Just hold me, she whispers.

I can feel her bones. Nothing left of her. Is this what it comes to? That if I do not love her, she is going to waste away?

I am shocked. Until now I have been blind to my wife's self neglect, so enmeshed in my own obsessions. I had always thought that if I ever had an affair, the marriage would be over, that she would simply never forgive me. I realise now that I don't know my wife at all.

So now I cannot guess what she might do. The thought scares me.

I cannot change for you, she told me once. If I do not accept her as she is, she will die. Yet I am unhappy. It is a stark choice.

As I climb into bed, I hate myself for this weakness, this compromise. I have gone to where it is safe and warm, but it is not where my heart wants to go.

For days after my return I drive aimlessly in the car, or sit in coffee shops reading newspapers, unable to concentrate on anything. I can't work at all. Anna has her work. She will bury her distress under the layers of projects in her in-tray.

Jen is impatient with me. Terry has begged to come home after his latest illicit liaison and she is feeling empowered again.

– She voted with her feet, she says, no nonsense, trying to make me see reason over vodka and orange in the snug of the Wheatsheaf.

– I thought she wanted passion and romance. Like me. She said she did.

– Men are always asking what women want. Do you know what women want, Mark?

– Tell me.

– Security. That's what she has with . . . . what's his name?

– Paul.

– He's there. He's never going to leave her. Not now. She has him where she wants him. You have to learn to think like a woman. You really are hopeless at this, aren't you? She spelled out the rules, if you were listening. You were the one that broke them, not her.

– I thought you all wanted love. Communication. Trust.

– Give me a break, Jen says.

* * *

Mark D'Arbanville

I am worried about Sue and move back home for a few days. I start thinking about compromise. Sue is in bad shape but I want somehow to keep Anna in my life.

The next day I send her an email.

Would you consider going back to what we had, be my soul mate and best friend and your secret lover, and no more than that? Never demanding more than enriching each other's lives in so many ways without disrupting them?

For me to bring you the things you don't find in the run of your life? A secret friend and lover who never demands more? Could I not yet make up what is missing in your life as you make up what is missing in mine?

She has prised apart my heart, like taking a knife to an oyster shell. Anna is too special in my life to let go.

I get her reply just an hour later.

I have read your email four times to date and will probably read it another ten times before the day is out. How do I feel? Elated. Scared. Excited. Feel I have my best friend back. I smiled for the first time in days. Wanted to make love to you straight away. Really wondered if we could do this without hurting yourself or Susan or me. Confused. Intense love.

We are crazy, mister, but I guess that is what drew us together. Do you think we could really do this?

Perhaps I should have walked away after that first time at Paddington Station. But then I think about all the times we would not have had and that makes me think of all the times I could still have, always there is the temptation of just one more time. But each time I fall in love with her even more and every moment spent together the wound goes a little deeper and now I cannot stem the bleeding.

I should not have come back to Susan. I think of it as damage control but it is only making it worse.

I cannot find my way out of the woods. But I do know how to get in deeper.

Mark D'Arbanille

Forty-one

In a marriage, having an affair is like putting a bandaid on a sucking chest wound. It's never just about the sex. Whether you admit it to yourself or not, the marriage is in real trouble.

You tell yourself: I can get here what I don't get at home, it will make things better, and perhaps it does, for a while, but then guilt and resentment start to eat away at you, like acid through the wire of a fuse. Either you have serial affairs, and your life becomes a lie; or you run from the guilt and end the affair. For a time it feels better living without the guilt, but then the discontent builds again, and you realise you didn't fix the problem when you ended the affair. Sooner or later the ground opens up beneath you because an affair is one step beyond denial and the one before realising it's wrecked.

Jen says it's having your cake and eating it.

Only there is no cake to eat. Just a few crumbs in either place.

It was no salve for Sue and I, it only drew aside the curtain on the gulf that had grown between us. Is this true for Anna and Paul? I cannot say, I do not know how they live. From the moment I wanted to leave Sue for her, Anna brought down the blinds. I was no longer an impartial friend.

For years I fought with Sue, thinking one day there would be a breakthrough, one day I would know how to fix this, or I would know for certain that it was time to leave.

For years we argued over *how* to live together; we never asked *why* we still lived together. If we had asked ourselves that question, some of the answers may have been clearer.

Or perhaps this was why we never asked.

Even now it is not yet clear to me why we have been loveless in our marriage for so long. But I will find out, and I will do it in the most painful and terrible way imaginable.

Mark D'Arbanville

Forty-two

Yet another trip down to London, business expenses taking a hammering this year. My accountant shakes his head and wonders what the hell is going on.

We are lying on the bed in a Kensington hotel room watching a delayed telecast of a Champions League football match between Manchester United and Real Madrid. I am Manchester United and I have told Anna she is Real Madrid because she looks more Spanish than me. We have worked out our own rules.

Offside is oral sex for one minute.

A tackle from behind: the injured team member lies face down on the bed and the offender massages them with their body.

A free kick is gentle fondling anywhere you want on your body for one whole minute.

A red card is a deep kiss, then the other player comes on their own while the red card watches.

A yellow card: the offender has their hands tied and the other player describes the best sex they have ever had with someone else while fondling the offender.

A goal means penetration during the celebrations and until the restart.

The winning team is rewarded with the orgasm.

Manchester United win 4-3.

Christ.

I still cannot see a linesman wave an offside flag without getting aroused.

Mark D'Arbanille

Forty-three

I am in my hotel room in Kensington and she is in their townhouse in Fulham with friends serving finger food. I am sore from making love with her and I know she is sore also, and while she is laughing with the girlfriends and wives and the men sprawl on the sofa yelling at the English football team on the flickering television screen she will have an ache in her groin from where she is raw and yet I am the one who's jealous, because I am excluded from her normal life. I am her fantasy and no one ever sees me behind her eyes.

Everyone has a secret life, a world where no one else is allowed, a curtained theatre behind the eyes where dark secrets play. We chip away at loneliness when we invite selected guests for private showings. Anna lets these movies run when we are in bed, so that she is not like one woman, but a hundred. Sometimes there are also grainy and flickering newsreel images from the past, from her childhood, some ugly and painful, and the film flickers and runs off the spool as men walk threateningly towards the camera of her eye.

There are gauzy images from an imagined future with children and joy and peace. She could have had these things with Paul. That she doesn't gives the lie to Jen and her intimations of duplicity.

I look for reason in this and find none.

I am her dream lover. Every man's fantasy, except that it isn't, not for me. If it was just sex, she would not have fallen in love with me, or said the things she has said. So what does she really want, more than sex, more than passion, more than this eccentric and unconventional love affair?

More than a lover and best friend?

More than the most special man in the world?

The next day we meet at a pub near the Strand and sit in the beer garden. We are both tense.

– Why do you stay with him, Anna?

– He's all I've ever known, Mark.

– Is that it?

– He's kind. When I get in one of my rages, he never reacts. He's always gentle.

I want to say to her: is that it? Either she does not want to hurt me or she is lying through her teeth or she really is crazy.

I listen for intimations of passion and instead I have the impression of a lead-frame piano sitting there in the living room of her small apartment, too heavy and too expensive and too taxing to shift, and so it sits there year after year gathering dust, a beloved treasure she once thought she might like to play but which is now out of tune.

This must be a lover's conceit, it cannot be the way it really is.

Mark D'Arbanille

– It's not just me, Mark. I've been as much a refuge from your life as you have been for me.

– What's the point of having a marriage if you need refuge from it?

The bewilderment leaves me defenceless. If I am her best friend, what is there left for Paul?

– How can you stay with him?

She looks at me over the rim of her wine glass and her expression changes from anguish to suspicion. Another man out to trap her.

– I'm the only one who really understands him.

– If you don't love him, what's the point?

– I thought we weren't going to do this.

It feels like a door slamming in my face. Her heart is like a shell, closing when it feels movement in the water, always vigilant.

– I don't understand you, Anna.

– I feel suffocated sometimes. You're both the same. You both pressure me for an answer and I can't breathe!

– I just want to know what you want, for Christ's sake!

– I never asked you to do any of this! she snaps, and she rushes off to the restroom, leaving me glowering at a glorious English summer afternoon. Why shouldn't I be jealous? Despite the agreement we have made, I want to be real in her life.

That night we meet at a screenwriters guild dinner in Chelsea. I flirt over roast duck with an attractive thirty-something documentary maker with huge hazel eyes, looking to elicit a response from Anna, who is glaring at me from the other side of the table.

As the party breaks up, I wait for her a hundred metres

from the restaurant. We can't be seen leaving together. She walks with me to the corner where I flag down a cab.

– Will you come back to the hotel with me?

– I can't.

– You don't have to tell him it's over. All you have to do is not go home one night. It's that easy. If that's what you want.

– I can't do that to him.

– But you can do it to me.

– And maybe I can't do this anymore! she says, and this is an Anna I have not seen before.

She gets in her cab and drives off, cold and angry. A black hole opens up underneath me.

I do not sleep at all that night and at dawn I am patrolling the ugly underbelly off Bayswater Road. The pavement is slick from early morning rain, warmed by a weak yellow sun. The huddled homeless sleep in shop doorways. I buy an early edition newspaper and stare at it, not reading a word, seven in the morning and disgusted with life.

I want to crawl under a blanket in a shopfront stoop, join the loveless and desperate in their vigil, among the scarlet-lipped women in anoraks offering parodies of love for the angry and displaced.

It is a looking glass world that makes no sense at all. I walk back to my hotel, unshaven and hollowed out.

She is waiting, shivering, in the street.

– Where have you been? she says.

I look up. I can't believe it's her. She looks forlorn, eyes red-rimmed with tears.

– I looked for you everywhere.

Mark D'Arbanville

How can she love me so much when she still lives with Paul?

– I'm sorry about last night, I murmur.

– Why do you want me to be jealous of you? I hate jealousy.

– It's normal.

– It's what Michael did, she says, invoking the name of the actor who first broke her heart. He drove me mad with it, I swore I'd never be jealous of anyone again. How can I be jealous of anything you do when I'm living with another man?

– You don't think I'm jealous of Paul? It tears me to bits.

– That's what I've been telling you. You shouldn't love me so much. Find some woman who will love you properly.

But that is no longer the point. I don't want someone who will love me, I need someone I can love back, so I don't make the same mistakes again. A lover and a best friend.

If Susan cannot be that, if I cannot love her that way, then it is time to let her go, take my hands off the wheel, and let life take over.

Forty-four

I know Anna doesn't want me, that there is no hope there. But this is not about Anna anymore. After all, I knew in my heart I would never let myself have Anna, despite Jen's glib summation of my behaviour. If I ever left Sue, I would have to punish myself by giving up Anna as well.

That is the way a lifetime of guilt has led me to think.

I have never learned the difference between love and guilt. As Jen said to me once, I would have made a very fine Catholic.

Mark D'Arbanille

Forty-five

Back in Manchester I ring Sue and tell her I have to see her.

We sit down in my study, and I close the door. Framed film posters jostle for space on the walls, screenplays I wrote, back in another life when I was happy and successful. It feels like such a long time ago.

The look on her face. Guilt is like God's accusing finger. I can hardly breathe for the shame.

It is as if I am standing outside myself, watching, a crippled man trying to walk. I stare at one of the posters: it is a close-up of a woman with an anguished expression, in sepia tones. The movie was called *Loss*. Once, what I created was imaginary.

– It's over, Sue.

– We can try again.

It's unthinkable that she should still want me after my affair with Anna, everything I have done calculated to make her let me go. I had thought to find the limit of her needing of me and have not.

Friends have told her to get on with her life and to hell with that bastard you married. They have told her she will be fine without me.

– I can't, Sue.

– I don't think I can live without you, Mark.

– I just can't do this anymore.

She stands and touches my arm, lightly. There are hot tears in her eyes. She is breaking in front of me.

This is unbearable.

– We can't let this go, Mark. It's too much to throw away.

She's right, there is so much we have shared together. But if I go back now it will only be to rescue her, and she doesn't want to be rescued, she wants to be loved, and admired, and valued.

I do not want to be responsible for her happiness, or for anyone's. There has to be some other way that a marriage can work.

This is what it must be like to be a user, one of those pitiful creatures in the city slumped beside a rubbish skip. Neither of us will let the needle slip to the floor, even though our addiction to this marriage is destroying us both.

One of the partners where she works is a friend. He has rung, worried for her. She is by nature a meticulous and obsessively organised woman. Lately she has become argumentative and slipshod.

I hesitate.

But for all my doubts – and there are many – I know

I cannot go back to that life. I feel something inside me clench tight like a fist. As the saying goes, my heart is just not in it anymore.

I think what my life would be like if I stayed, if Anna was consigned to a speed bump in the marriage, and we return to the old ways. I know I may not have the strength to come to this again.

– After all we've been through, Mark. I can change. I can help you change.

– I don't want you to change for me. I don't want to change for you.

Before today I have always wilted in the face of her sorrow. Now I break the pattern of a lifetime. I have to trust that there will be happiness on the other side of this for me and for her. I am too exhausted to go on like this.

Even if I can't have Anna, I want the man Anna showed me I might one day become. I have been faking this for too long. If I cannot do this right, it's better to be on my own. It scares the hell out of me. But we'll destroy each other if I stay.

– I can't live without you, Mark. I don't know what I'll do.

Time freezes. The threat is implicit. I always feared responsibility, now I have been handed the ultimate trust.

– I just can't do this anymore, Sue.

I step away from the anchors of a lifetime, into the darkness.

Forty-six

David Beckham's haircut dominates everything. As in life. There are posters everywhere. The blinds are drawn and my son has his back to me and is staring at the computer screen. He is playing Sims, manipulating fictional computer people the way he cannot control his reality.

There are CD-ROMs scattered over the carpet, along with maths books, a bicycle helmet and a deflated soccer ball.

I sit down in the chair next to him.

– David . . .

– Were you and Mum fighting again?

– We're trying to work things out.

Even now I cannot tell him the truth.

– Why don't you come home?

– David, I can't.

– Why not?

– Will you turn off that computer and look at me?

He ignores me.

Mark D'Arbanille

– Turn off the computer!

He pauses the game and crosses his arms, still staring at the screen.

– You're killing Mum. You and that bitch in London.

– That bitch in London wants me to come home to you. I'm the one that wants to leave. And I'm not leaving you, David. I just . . . this marriage . . .

– You're such a fucking dickhead.

Rage leaves me breathless.

– What did you just say?

– You're not here anymore, why do I have to be nice to you?

– Because I'm your dad.

– You don't give a shit about us!

His chair crashes back onto the floor. He is on his feet now. Sue comes in and stands between us, stop it, stop it. I storm out.

– You'll not see me again, I shout, forever melodramatic. I feel overwhelmed with guilt and frustration, think I'll drive my car into a tree, get this over with.

But I am right about one thing. It is the last time she ever sees me. I ring next morning to apologise to David, but there is no answer and when I get there, she's gone, there is just a note on the kitchen bench saying she's gone to stay with a girlfriend in Manchester. I think nothing of it, don't even keep the note, which, as it transpires, is her last letter to me but one.

Forty-seven

The night we met.

I turn from the bar and she is there, and we start talking, as if we have known each other a lifetime. She is smiling into my eyes and I know something is happening, very fast. Her eyes are bright and dancing, there is an energy to her and a lightness, and my shyness evaporates in the warmth of her.

The bar is crowded and so we arrange to meet in a jazz club later. I go for the burn. By one o'clock that morning we are French kissing on the dance floor of a nightclub, and a week later we are sleeping together.

There has only been one lover for her before this. She lost her virginity in the back of a Volkswagen and her only impression of sex, she said, was the one the gearstick made in the small of her back.

There are hot summer nights in my Richmond bedsit when we both lose our inhibitions pouring Asti Spumante on each other's bodies and licking it off. She laughs a lot. In those days she knew how to laugh.

One night she is sitting on my lap in the front room of her parents' house. We have been going out for less than three weeks. She tells me she loves me and I feel not joy, but panic.

– Tell me you love me, she says.

I have never told any woman I love her. What is love anyway? I have no idea.

– I know you do, she says.

There is a stone in my throat, a tight iron band around my chest.

– I'm not getting up until you say it, she says, and she means it.

I cannot make the words come out of my mouth. I sit there for an hour and she does not get up and finally I say the words: I tell her I love her.

Segue to a hotel room in a tiny Oxfordshire village a lifetime later, looking into Anna's eyes when these same words slip out, unbidden. *I love you.*

From such moments relationships are forever defined.

The gypsies have a saying: *the first one to say I love you, loses.*

Forty-eight

It is the bravest thing and the worst thing. The police find her two days later in a bed and breakfast – the Country Rest – an hour's drive from Hanford. She has booked in under the name Susan Robinson – her name before she married me.

When I tell David what has happened he tries, literally, to climb the walls. The doctor is called, gives him sedatives. I sit with Greg and remember curling into a foetal position on the living room carpet. It is like a hand has closed around my viscera and is shaking me from the inside, I am physically breathless with grief. This is unthinkable.

Thoughts windmill around inside my head. I will have to face her family, the village, the school. Why did she do this? Was it desperation, was it revenge?

How will I survive this?

How will David?

The next day I go into the mortuary room at the hospital. I am afraid to touch her. She looks like a toppled statue.

Mark D'Arbanille

Her skin is marbled and there is a crystalline tear frozen on her cheek.

Guilt clutches his brute fist around my heart and his fingers sink in to the first knuckle.

David is waiting for me in the corridor outside. There are no words for him.

Forty-nine

She went away with Paul that weekend, to a hotel in Chichester, trying to repair her marriage. I plan to lie to her, tell her I don't want to see or hear from her again. Make her hate me so she stays away and is not touched by this. A close friend talks me out of it.

– I'll ring her, he says. Don't talk to her now, don't do anything while you're like this, you're not thinking straight. She's going to find out sooner or later. But you have to tell her the truth, you owe her that much.

The truth. What a rare commodity.

Fifty

I sit in the cold black house and watch the flickering images and sounds of another time. She is there on the VCR, holding David, who is just a few months old. She looks up at me and with a familiar flash of irritation from across the years wants to know if I have the recorder running. She keeps asking, over and over, her irritation out of proportion. Where did all this anger come from?

I remember two years before this film was taken, a sparse flat, a typewriter, no lounge, a collage on the fridge, dreams cut from a magazine pasted on.

– If I just had a baby, I'd be happy.

I have left a well paid job as a copywriter with Saatchi & Saatchi and Susan has just discovered she is pregnant. I am thinking about going back to the industry and giving up my dream, but she believes I can do this. I sit at the kitchen table writing comedy scripts. Every Tuesday I have to be funny or we don't eat, but we have each other, and I think it makes our relationship strong.

I sell my first television series, and get funding for a film treatment. Somehow we get through. David is born. He is wonderful. We both love him desperately.

But it doesn't make her happy.

Something shifts when David arrives. This relationship was never designed to weather such a sea change. The marriage drifts, rudderless and demasted, but neither of us will abandon her.

– *If I just had a baby, I'd be happy.*

In truth, there was only one person who could make Susan happy, and four days ago she left the building.

Mark D'Arbanville

Fifty-one

I turn off the VCR and go outside onto the patio, into the bright sunshine.

The ficus growing in an old wine barrel has become pot bound, the roots have fingered through the bricks. I lever it off the paving with a crowbar. It is slowly dying, there is no room to grow.

That's what happened to us.

I wander through the house like a ghost, restless and disconnected. There is so much to arrange for the funeral but my mind drifts away. I cannot even remember what I was doing five minutes ago. I get up with purpose and seconds later cannot remember why.

I sit down at her bureau, open and close the drawers, stare blankly at the little post-it notes she wrote to herself, at inspirational quotes she saved to get her through the dark times. Not inspirational enough, as it turned out. The oiled wood has a fragrance to it that I associate particularly with her.

I find a blind cabinet and slide the door open. There are three journals, haphazardly filled, two have soft leather covers and smooth white vellum paper, the other is cheaper and spiral bound. I open this one gingerly as if it is primed to explode, let it fall open in the middle, to a day perhaps a year before our separation.

What is wrong? Why is this happening? Didn't I always do the right thing, wasn't I always the good wife, a good mother, arrange the dinner parties, wasn't I always the good girl?

But I didn't want a good girl, I want to shout into the silence. Or maybe once I did, when I was up there on that pedestal. But when she shook me off, I realised I wanted someone a little more earthy.

There is a letter folded into the pages, addressed to me, a letter I never received.

So hard to know where to start, how far back to go.
Our life together has seemed like a battle to me: I have felt under siege. I have erected battlements to protect myself against which you have fought, trying to break them down.
I feel as though I have been starved out, starved of your total love and affection. I've waited for complete admiration, not most of it. So in response to your criticisms I built these battlements and over many years this bloody castle has stood. Implacable

Mark D'Arbanville

and stubborn and I guess anticipating battles that never ever happened.

I am angry at you for hurting me, that you and your needs being met were more important than anything else. I'm angry at your selfishness that drove you to improve me or have all of me no matter what the cost.

But the price was me. Sometimes angry and retaliating, sometimes wounded and bleeding. But both meant the battlements went higher until three weeks ago when I guess I had no more energy to build the walls higher and you too saw the futility of trying to get through.

I have loved you less for this.

But ultimately as much as I am hurt and angered by how you tried to control me, I am most hurt at me for allowing you to do it all these years. And thank God for the energy to defend my walls vanished. How angry I am at me for letting me get to this point.

I have felt like I am in some sort of breakdown. Just wanting to sleep so I don't hurt anymore.

I should have walked away from those battlements long ago. Allowing myself to be under siege for so long was a travesty . . .

I let the paper slip through my fingers to the floor.

If this was how she felt, why did she go on with it? Why did I? The truth was, I felt I couldn't leave, that it was my duty to stay. And where would I run to? I never had any idea what a guiltless relationship looked like, if moving on would not mean the same thing with someone else. Besides, I was terrified of being alone, and so I tortured her by staying but never really loving her enough.

The way I loved her, the only way I knew then, was as her protector and mentor. Or that's how I saw it. I never let down my guard, let her see me as I was, that wasn't my role.

Over the years I tried to change her into the woman I could be in love with, into an Anna.

We called it a marriage. As justification I looked around, in the football club, at the pub, and saw other men doing exactly the same thing and that made it all right.

In the end, love became the avoidance of guilt.

Susan did not get what she needed from me, her fear of being abandoned so great she was just as trapped as I was.

All that time spent reading new age books with catchy titles, seeing marriage counsellors, trying to improve our communication skills, when really it was this: we were two people stuck in the same lift.

So when we finally walked away from each other Susan's fortress came tumbling right down, undermined from within as well as without.

Mark D'Arbanville

Fifty-two

In every life there are moments that bring it definition.

I remember Susan once told me how, when she was seven years old, the family were getting ready to go to on a picnic in the car. Her six other siblings, four brothers, two sisters, piled into the family Vauxhall. Susan, desperate for attention, hid under the bed, expecting her parents to come and find her.

Lying there, curled up with the musty smell of the dusty carpet, she waited for her mother's panicked voice, her father's urgent calls. Where is she? Where's Susan?

But they didn't come.

The next thing little Susan remembered was hearing the car reverse out of the driveway. They had driven off without her.

It was a big family after all. Perhaps her parents were fighting. It was a hot day and I can imagine six kids squabbling and yelling, it would have been bedlam inside the car. Perhaps they realised Sue was missing as soon as they reversed out of the driveway. The abandonment may have lasted no more than a few minutes.

She could never remember.

What she did remember was that this was her reward for being the good girl, the undemanding one, the quiet one, the one who always helped and never caused trouble and never asked for anything for herself.

Years later, her husband rewarded her this same way. Strange how we replay our childhood horrors in our adult life, conjure our pain from the past until we resolve it.

In her husband's defence he faced a stark choice. He could stay and rescue her from under that bed, knowing in later life he could never give her what she so rightfully demanded of him; or he could try and be a better man elsewhere.

Love as rescue. It kills people.

Mark D'Arbanville

Fifty-three

I open one of the journals. The first entry I find is from Valentine's Day, the year before: *Dear God, I guess more than anything I feel lost and alone . . .*

It is getting dark. I turn on a table lamp next to my chair.

Mark has put a Valentine's Day special on the fridge, from Toby's restaurant. I feel so mean if I don't go along with it, would it really hurt to let him think he's a great guy for thinking of it? It's a farce. He doesn't think about it any other time and really what's the point?

But all this important stuff inside of me is being pushed down because I don't feel able to talk to anyone, the greater the turmoil, the greater the need to appear normal.

I have withdrawn emotionally because he cannot, will not, fill that need for me. This has always been the flaw in us . . . he may not have me in any deep sense but he does still have me, in ways that don't demand much of him . . . we get along, we talk on safe topics, we have sex and we seem OK like that . . . it's not OK for me but it seems OK for him . . .

I'm just treading water for a while, giving myself breathing space because I feel very confused. I have lost my sense of self.

Mark said to me today that the only solid thing in our lives right now was our relationship. He is uninspired at work, and worried what will happen when David leaves. Oh God of all things I didn't think he thought our relationship was great. Thankfully I had sunglasses on and he couldn't see the disbelief in my eyes. So my withdrawing my emotional life from us and being outwardly fine and having sex when he wants which I do freely and happily but never initiate is all it takes to have a great relationship. Fuck! There are too many uncertainties in my life to put US back on the agenda. I feel very sad and alone as though I'm walking in this foreign land where nobody sees me or understands my language.

It's Valentine's Day tomorrow and let's hope Mark does nothing because there might be sex and superficial talk. We are united as parents but there is no romance or deep abiding love.

Mark stormed out shouting that if he lived to be a hundred he'll never understand women!

Well he got that much right!

Mark D'Arbanville

I take a bottle of bourbon down to the brook at the bottom of the lane and stand shivering in my shirtsleeves, in the pitch dark. I choke up whatever is in my stomach before I even touch the bottle. Cold stars wheel across the sky. Wind rushes through the grass.

I do not recognise this man in the journals, except that it happens to be me.

Oh, Sue. She had always been the perfect wife, her mum's good little girl. It tore her apart, being a good girl, fixing everyone else first. There never was space for her.

Fifty-four

Her name was Mary and Susan adored her. She sometimes referred to her as a saint.

Mary was born to a well bred and well connected mill family outside Bolton, not far from Manchester. Much was made of her making a good marriage, as they called it then. But the good marriage she made was only good from her father's point of view.

Mary made the youthful mistake of falling in love. He was a Protestant boy by the name of Frank Young, from a working class family. He was a foreman at her father's mill.

Mary's father had no intention of ever allowing his daughter to make such a disgusting union. When he discovered what she had been doing he forbade Mary to ever see Frank again.

Soon after they took her away for a weekend to a Lake District hotel. A week taking the airs was considered a salve for Mary's broken heart. It was in the hotel's dining room one afternoon, while taking tea, that she was introduced to Richard, well bred, well educated, and well turned out. His father owned a textile factory in Manchester. The inference in family lore was that her family had arranged this meeting in order to take Mary's mind off her unsuitable boy.

Mary went along with it, perhaps feeling it was futile to resist life and fate, and they married a year later. Richard was a decent man, but conservative and emotionally remote. Mary soon learned to hate him. She had missed her chance at passion and her revenge took the form of martyrdom: *look what you did to me.*

Mary got by on five year plans. She would stick out the marriage for this long, until she had saved enough money to leave; if things had not improved, she would go. Things did not improve but she always found another reason to stay, usually because there was another child.

After thirty years, with all the children gone and a chance of freedom if she wanted it, she happened into Frank once more in a furniture store in Liverpool. He was married, of course, with three children. Looking into her former lover's face, she saw a lifetime of regret, both hers, and his.

She went home and tried to take her own life with pills.

After Mary came out of hospital, one of Sue's sisters helped her mother arrange the divorce. Mary never again spoke to Richard, who never understood why.

Sue became her mother's daughter, as perhaps every daughter does until she finds a way to break the chain. What were the facts of Susan's life in the end? She was a good girl who learned to compromise, who did her duty by her family, and lived with a man who became emotionally remote from her. Instead of leaving, she stayed until it was too late.

Mary was not a saint, of course. She was an ordinary woman who loved her children but who unintentionally taught her daughters that compromise was inevitable. The pattern that follows every family is inexorable. She did not do this by anything she said but, as all parents do, by the life she lived.

And if imitation is the way we show love, Sue remained loyal to her mother to the end.

Mark D'Arbanville

Fifty-five

The funeral home has worked from a photograph in applying her make-up. She looks like a waxwork image of herself, and the post-mortem has wrought subtle changes in her features.

David shakes his head and backs away: *that's not my mum.*

I reel back also. Nothing in my whole life has prepared me for this.

Mark and I have grown apart. We have moments that recapture what we once valued but we can't sustain it. I spent enormous energy redecorating his study. I guess I would have loved it if I had spent that energy on a room of my own.

We talk about David, his work, my work, but nothing on a deeper level. It is basic and superficial but it puts no pressure on us so actually it works out OK. I need someone to talk to about my fears, my

issues, my life. What we have is not the relationship
I want but I can't make him give something he is
not capable or not willing to give.

Mark seems contented enough, the problem seems
to be mine. We are wary friends with some sex.

It's funny how you can travel along and to all
appearances be OK and then suddenly you lose the
focus and you're not OK. I feel disconnected and so
tired and I guess it's the pretence. Our relationship
seems so poor and barren. The distance between us is
vast, given his aversion to in-depth conversations.

My aversion to in-depth conversations. I wonder what Anna would say if she read that. Why could I be the man Sue wanted only with another woman?

I do not know the answer to this, not yet. So instead I silently mount a defence against the armies of my accusers. I was there for her, wasn't I? Through all those fights, all the frustration, I never left.

Until eight months ago, when I met Anna.

It seems now there was as much frustration as fighting. Because we didn't scream at each other every single night we kept everyone fooled, even ourselves. What there was, for me, was a constant and nagging feeling of desperation, an emotional toothache that set us for ever on edge.

We coped by creating distance between us, there were friends or family or David or work, Sue had yoga and tennis and book clubs, nothing wrong with any of this except they weren't outside interests, they were a means of refuge.

Mark D'Arbanville

So was it a kindness to stay, then? Or was it not more true that I made this moment daily more inevitable? A marriage has to be more than damage control.

David will not go near the open coffin. There are no goodbyes. These will come later, after forgiveness, after too much pain.

I see Mary moving silently in the back pews, with the other ghosts in this room. My own childhood is a part of this also, of course, and led me inevitably here.

Fifty-six

My grandfather had a window cleaning round in the East End of London that he sold at the pub for three pints of beer. He violently abused my grandmother until the day she hit him over the head with a skillet as he was eating his sausages at the dinner table.

He never touched her again.

My own mother created a haven for me, away from the violence and the poverty she had endured. I was Ivy's golden-haired boy; but favourite sons grow up with an inflated sense of their own self importance as well as feeling so drained by the experience they have no sense of self worth at all.

She married a man least like her bullying, violent father. He was a gentle man who never displayed a moment of anger in his entire life. His name was George and I harboured for him an undying affection and endless frustration. I wanted a father who could be my mentor and friend, a buffer between me and my mother's cloying love.

Mark D'Arbanville

But my father was never around, he spent his life on the road, a glib and successful salesman with few real friends who spent his love on barmaids and divorcees. My mother found comfort for her bruised heart with the one lover who was available to her always, the one male in the family who could not abandon her.

Me.

Sometimes when I was a little boy she hugged me so tight I could not breathe; her love was like that.

I escaped when I was eighteen to go to Leeds University to study English. I remember how she sobbed on my shoulder at the train station. It was like disengaging from an octopus.

I always loved women, but experience had taught me they were dangerous. There was only one way to handle them, as I handled my own mother: you took care of the ones who idolised you, but you never let them get too close.

Love meant being responsible for someone else's happiness. Love meant intolerable burdens. I did not want to be alone, but I didn't want responsibility either. It was a paradox, of course, which is why my life ended up such a mess.

And I was right all along, about love, wasn't I? Hadn't Susan just proved the consequences of loving someone?

You can run all your life but at some time you have to turn and face your demons.

Fifty-seven

The night before the funeral I have a dream about her.
We are in Innsbruck, on a skiing holiday with David and Deb,
Sue's sister, two years before. We are sitting together in the
hot spa in the garden, with a distant view of white-capped
mountains.

I have her journal from back then:

> *My back feels like it's going to break, it's the load I'm*
> *carrying around with me. My back is breaking*
> *because I can't bear this weight anymore . . .*

– What's wrong, Mark?

I can barely look at her and I do not know why I am
so angry.

– I feel frozen, I say.

– What is it?

What is it? It's the matronly clothes she wears. It's the

sacrifice. It's that she never makes me jealous, but she knows how to make me feel guilty. It's that we never laugh together anymore. It's that I feel as if we are twenty years older than we really are.

– I don't know what it is, I tell her, because I can't tell her the truth without knowing how to fix the problem.

I don't feel valued and truly loved for who I am.

I never knew she felt this way back then. Even if I had had the journal at the time, it would have made no difference. I remember the fights, going round and round in circles. We called it progress.

I seem to feel so frightened to share this stuff with Mark, because I don't feel he listens to me, don't feel he likes to examine all this stuff, I feel I need to do that to understand it, and let it go.

This stuff has gone through our whole relationship. It certainly was in the open after David was born but I honestly suspect that it was present in the very beginning.

I feel weak and a failure because I couldn't explain to him how much this was hurting me. In trying to satisfy him, I have hurt myself more than he ever could because I let him do this to me.

It seems to me I've spent my whole life just trying to please those I love.

Fifty-eight

– **I never wanted** to marry the two of you.

Strong words from a priest, especially now, before I am about to step inside the church to speak the eulogy for my wife.

– She was always too needy of you, he says. You never let her stand on her own two feet. I never thought it would last.

– Why didn't you tell us, Peter?

– I did. I told Susan.

Too needy of you. I remember once, before we were married, we were living back in London then. I had to go to Birmingham for a client pitch. The second night, when I was at dinner in the hotel restaurant with the creative director and our prospective clients, I was given a message that my wife was at reception.

– I don't have a wife, I mutter before excusing myself and getting the lift down to the foyer. Sue has driven all the way up the M1 and is sitting miserably on the banquette opposite reception, clutching a wet Kleenex in her fist, saying she cannot be without me, and I say, but it has only been two nights. Later I see the look on my boss's face: *you've got problems there.*

She stands by me when I leave my job to risk my hand as a scriptwriter, and believes in me when no one else does. I need *her* then and it is the best time of our life together.

I always believed that taking care of Susan was somehow my duty, this was the standard I judged myself by. When someone needs you, they cannot leave you. But the flip side is, you cannot leave them either. When it later becomes unworkable there is no way out.

I remember the crucifix in the local church when I was six or seven years old, a man suffering torture so that everyone else might be happy. I grew up thinking that suffering was somehow noble, that martyrdom was what God wanted. But now the man who married us is telling me that sadness and sacrifice were signs that I was living the wrong sort of life.

– You can only be good for others if you're good for yourself, Mark. It's like a ripple in a pond. Happiness spreads out. So does unhappiness.

His words haunt me on this the unhappiest day of my life. Every seed of misery will one day grow fruit, no matter how long ago it was planted.

Fifty-nine

In the afternoon at two o'clock I bury my wife. There are no words for this.

There is a white coffin before the altar. I walk into the church and feel the eyes of the village on me. David will not hold my hand, will not touch me.

He speaks a private eulogy to her with a dignity and endurance that sets me trembling for him.

> *I feel so vulnerable, I don't want to be alone, I've been born into the middle of a big family and built my life around a safe haven. My fear of being alone is so great and so terrifying. If I gave Mark the power to make decisions about who or what I am then the implicit agreement is that he'll look after me and I won't be alone ever.*

As the coffin leaves the chapel, they play 'You'll Never Walk

Mark D'Arbanville

Alone'. It was her favourite song. But she did walk alone in the end, we all do.

A short ride to the crematorium, mostly in silence. A summer's day, grey and overcast. A drizzle of rain.

Inside the crematorium we watch the coffin disappear through the curtain. Then I join the other mourners outside and we release balloons into a leaden sky, over the black waters of the lake.

> *I have needed to discuss my fears and issues and talk through it but this has never happened. I was suffering personally for it and punishing Mark because I didn't see him fulfilling his side of things. It has never worked in our relationship and my persistence has only left me frustrated, hurt, angry, withdrawn.*

The day ends quickly, chill and damned. Dying this way throws shadows over lives in ways that cannot be imagined.

> *I need to accept the reality of this and find a better way. So either I continue knowing that it is not, has not, and never will work or ACCEPT the reality and find other ways. Letting go includes the illusions that I have had about our relationship and the ideal that communication between us should be open and a two way street.*

Susan was right. It should be open, it should be a two way street.

So what have you learned today, in farewelling this beautiful if flawed woman, this woman with whom you have shared so much of your life? This wonderful mother, this good friend?

I have learned that if you fake your life it will kill you slowly, terribly and cause the most pain for everyone. You try to do the right thing, not hurt anyone, conform to what love is supposed to be and what it is supposed to look like, but in the end it destroys you. It eats away at your heart and soul like acid. You slowly destroy those around you that you say you love, and you slowly destroy yourself.

This is what I did, and perhaps what she did, and this is the lesson I have learned here today.

Mark D'Arbanille

Sixty

Everyone has gone and I am alone again in the echoing house. Thank God I am alone. The village has been divided by this, a hung jury. Susan's friends would like to cut my balls off, some have said this. I cannot live here anymore, that much is clear.

I fetch the journals and, inevitably, the bourbon, and sit down in the den.

> *After mum died I sat with her and shared my grief*
> *over my relationship with Mark . . .*

Had it really been so long? If it had not been for these journals I would not have known. I gaze over a panorama of wasted time, waiting for things to get better, thinking if I could communicate better I could fix this.

> *I want us to tell David together about our difficulties*

and the respite of separate rooms. He wouldn't do it
so I had to do it on my own. Of course he already
knew. He took it well but Mark was so angry.

I was angry because it was not part of the perfect picture. I did not want to be real, I was the one who fixed everyone else's problems, I could not be vulnerable in the face of my own family, my friends, and especially my own son.

I feel I am reaching a point where I feel I will lose
myself, my integrity, the nucleus that is essentially me
if I do not say 'enough'.

I check the date. Three years since she wrote that. And she did not say enough. She kept trying to find a way to my muddled heart instead.

This is what separate bedrooms was about for
me. Telling Mark clearly I was not prepared to
compromise myself any more than I had. I need to
make the right choices and decisions for ME and that
may or may not ultimately affect the outcome of my
marriage. But either way the preservation of myself is
paramount to the survival of my wellbeing.

But she did not do it. And three years and five months later I left, and eight months after that she was dead.

Mark D'Arbanville

I have lost confidence, I want to stay home, I hate socialising, I am tired all the time, I love sleep because I can forget all this because I'm not being true to myself. I am trying to create myself into something I don't want, don't feel comfortable about and don't even understand. Ultimately this will never work no matter how much I try because if the needs of one person in a relationship hurt the other person then it can't possibly sustain itself, which is what I see has happened to us but tonight for the first time I understand why.

And no longer is David or Mark my most primary concern, I AM, otherwise I'll lose me forever.

The last sentence echoes in my head like the crashing of thunder.

We're living in the same house, Mark and I, but there is no lasting intimacy. I don't honestly have any inclination to share with my husband, he and I are on really different wavelengths. We go through the motions each day but there doesn't seem to be anything to sustain us. I could have come home early yesterday but David has a job at the supermarket now and it scared me to just have the two of us in the house.

Christ. This was two years before we separated.

I only know that there is stuff I need to talk about
and I scrawl it all down as it comes into my mind
free to say what I feel but I can't do that to Mark.
  It's not about Mark, or David leaving or Mum
dying. It's about what is happening to me inside.
I am dying because the way I have lived for the last
forty years is not working anymore.

If she had left me then, she might have survived. Why did she hold on, even after I met Anna, even after I left? Why did she ring Anna and tell her we had a wonderful marriage when she had been miserable in it for years?

Did she think there was nothing to her except her mum's good little girl? To the end she was loyal; she did what Mary did, she stayed in an unhappy marriage, because that's what a good girl does.

Whatever the reason, she stalled her decision, and then found she had left it too late.

She was a good woman, a true friend and a devoted mother. The only person she ever hurt was herself. Tonight it seems to me that she speaks for married women everywhere, and her plaintive whispers follow me sibilant through the empty, shadowed house.

With David for the past fifteen years, with Mark
before that and with Mum and Dad before that
I have shaped my life in being what I thought was
expected of me, a great Mum who was always there,
a great wife who was there for Mark, a great

Mark D'Arbanille

daughter who was there for Mum. I did this but at
the price of never being there for myself, or at the cost
of being so busy with everything else that I never had
time for me. I have desperately tried to cling on to
the external people in my life who have defined who
I am rather than face the frightening prospect of
having to define me for myself. My work has defined
me and without it I don't know who I'd be anymore.
I have to trust and listen to the voice inside. I know
I'll continue to die inside and begin to die outside if
I don't do this.

I shut the journal. There is nothing more to be said.

Sixty-one

And this was the road that led me here to this stark hospital bed, these monitors and respirators, this receiving room between life and death.

I imagine Anna might like her situation here; it is perfect distance. She is here, yet she is not, she can exist inside her own head, in morphine dreams, no one can hurt her. She is on the danger list and she is safe.

She has taken refuge in coma; here she is guiltless, faultless and responsible for no one. If she dies they must all look after themselves and it will not be her fault what happens to them. She has nothing more to live up to; even life itself is hers for the choosing.

But for this moment their attention is focused not on Anna, or their own misery, but on me. They are still waiting for me to speak . . .

Mark D'Arbanville

Sixty-two

For many the shock and grief of Susan's death ended with the funeral. For me, for David, it goes on and on.

I cannot think, I cannot work, and I cannot sleep. I cannot go anywhere or do anything to get away from this grief. I am raw, lonely, desperate and tired. Pain leaves me ragged and weak.

My fingers hover over Anna's number on the cell phone. I want to ring, but cannot.

I have never lost anyone that I loved; I had imagined that grief came like a rockfall, sudden and crushing, a disaster from which you slowly picked your way out.

But it's not that. Grief is a guerilla war, with daily losses and occasional catastrophic strikes, that goes on and on for years – as I later discover – until I wonder if it will ever end.

I am ambushed driving in the car, assailed on an empty country road by choking grief, and I have to pull over until it passes. I find an old photograph in a drawer while I am looking for socks and suddenly I am curled up on the carpet as if shot in the guts. For God's sake. I am stalked by grief, not only for Sue, but for all the lost dreams, and the lost past.

I fight with David over every little thing, even the choice of TV channel. Once he hurls the remote at me with such force it shatters on the brick wall. In the car we shout at each other because he is endlessly surfing radio stations and irritation turns quickly into trembling fury. I pull over and he gets out of the car screaming at me and calling me a knobhead fucker. My son, the linguist.

We are both as raw as phosphorus burns.

The pain is so unbearable I rush to move on. I have the promise of refuge with Anna, she keeps me from despair.

I deal with Sue's death in many ways; tell myself I didn't love her, rage at her for abandoning David and sabotaging my life, hate her for what this will do to Anna. It keeps the tidal wave of remorse dammed and at bay for now.

The depth of my grief is unexpected; after all, I wanted to leave the marriage, and leave her. I always thought that grief and personal loss were the same.

I have not written since the separation, we are living off savings. I cannot sit down for longer than a few minutes. Sleep is impossible. Every waking moment I feel as if I'm going to vomit. I walk kilometres every day, head down, lost in my own grim reflections. I'm always short of breath, though medical checks show that I am in the best of health.

My parents, my brother, my friends are desperately worried but I talk to no one. I turn inside, like a dog dragging itself to a dark corner of the wood shed to lick its wounds.

Mark D'Arbanville

David has gone back to boarding school at Roxton, forty miles away. He cannot bear even to look at me. Among his last words to me before he boards the bus: *you murdered my mum.*

There is a part of me that agrees with him, but not quite in the way he means. He is thinking about the last eight months. I am thinking about the last ten years.

That first night I sit in his bedroom, on his bed, staring at David Beckham's ponytail and drinking neat bourbon. Wondering how the fuck I got here.

Sixty-three

Six months pass. Time heals all wounds, they say. How much time? And how do they know?

Anna and I arrange to meet again in Paris. She has told Paul she is organising financing for a joint project with a French television company. He never questions her about anything. It is harder for her now because she is the only one that has to lie.

But guilt is starting to bite. On the phone she sounds strained and torn. She sends an email.

I have no news for you and I know this will make
you angry – I am battling through, just . . . and
I know that I am getting there slowly. I will not go
into the New Year like this. I am complicated, but
you know so are you, I tear you apart but you have
also done this to me.

I wish I could still talk to you, laugh with you,
but I know this is not what you want, need or

Mark D'Arbanville

deserve. I often wish that I could have one of our
holidays back, or to look forward to and just live
that moment you came to London – does it always
have to be so black and white, either I do this or
nothing? I know this is reality but reality is that we
will all die and we won't know when this is.

She haunts me, Mark, and I look at Paul and
I remember the betrayal and the lies and I look at
you and see all the pain as well as happiness I
have brought.

OK so now you will be screaming at me well why
don't I change something – my answer is I don't
know but I don't want to tear you up any more.
I love you. Anna.

I spend Christmas alone in my house of ghosts. David
spends the holidays with a school friend in Preston.

Anna has Christmas with Paul and her family. I hate my
enforced exile from normal life, I feel more lonely this one
day than I have in my whole life.

A text from Anna:

One week tomorrow I am going to take you so high
u will be in ecstasy and we will be one.

New Year's Eve, I ring her, a finger pressed to my other ear,
the shrill laughter of women pouring out of a bar, deafening.
This year is going to be crap, I know it. My heart is missing
beats. I feel sick.

– So you want to come with me to Paris and then you don't know if you ever want to see me again? I shout at her down the line.

– I asked you if you were okay with this. You said you thought we could do this.

– I'm okay with it, I shout back. I am already convincing myself I will not think about the end.

– I'll see you tomorrow, I say.

– Are you sure we can do this? she asks again.

I know I will lose her and there is nothing I can do about it.

Mark D'Arbanville

Sixty-four

A jazz club on the Left Bank near the Notre Dame, the Trois Mailletz, a smoky cellar with bare brick walls, sweaty, humming with sex. We stand side by side on a ledge halfway up the stairs drinking beer from bottles.

I am in Paris with a beautiful woman, and I am in love. A wonderful affair. Just for tonight, everthing is perfect. I would not trade this moment for a whole Hollywood life.

Heading to Reims from Paris we drive into a blizzard, are cocooned in a whiteout of snowdrifts with no horizon. It is like the world of our affair, surreal and superheated.

We stop at a gas station and while I am paying for the fuel I see her hunched over the bonnet clearing ice off the windscreen with tweezers from her make-up bag. My heart lurches in my chest and I fall in love with her again. When I get back to the car she has cleared the driver's side of ice but she is shivering. She hates the cold so much.

This delicious, wonderful girl.

I love the crumpled blouses she never irons – I iron them for her – and the jackets with torn linings she never mends. I love her elegance and style and the safety pin hidden in her skirts. I love her gasped 'Excellent!' at any lewd suggestion of mine.

I want to retreat from her, and I want to squeeze her till she bursts. Tenderness and passion entwine like creepers around my heart. I blow hot breath into her small cold hands.

Something is aching inside me, always a little more of my heart opening up to her.

Desire. Wanting. Dread.

Mark D'Arbanville

Sixty-five

Once, walking through the dark Moet cellars in Reims, she wonders aloud how she might hold up under torture.

I speculate if this thought is erotic or if she really would like to know quite how strong she is, *how much can I take, how much can I endure, for Paul, for Mark, for my mum, my sisters?* It always seems to me that she cares about other people's pain before her own.

Or is it that she uses her pain to keep the world at a distance?

She thinks her selflessness a virtue, I think of it as the virus that is poisoning her life. I think about all the women I have known in my life, how they have all put other people's happiness before their own: Susan, Mary, Anna. Not one of them left a legacy of joy behind.

Ironic or just inevitable?

– Do you think I would break? she says, staring into one of the cold, damp cellars.

There is a method to enduring great pain. A friend who was in the SAS told me about it. You have to separate yourself from your body, and after a time the pain suffuses to a sort of euphoria. Professional torturers are warned to watch for it, wait until their victim returns from their separation before they start again.

It seems to me there is a dark reservoir of ancient pain in her, and when the torment is too great she drifts away from it, stands back, *look, my life is not so bad, really. Look at all the good things.*

You won't break me.

And of course her life is not bad, not at all. But it is not her life that is the problem for she is intelligent, sassy and well travelled; it is the pain she carries inside her that has blighted it.

– How do you think I would stand up under torture?

How to answer such a question? I know she would betray no one, even those who gave her up, would spit in defiance. But life is a patient and expert inquisitor. If you have secrets to tell, anything to hide at all, he will break you in the end. He has all the time in the world and the longer you hold out, the more refined and excruciating the torments become.

Mark D'Arbanville

Sixty-six

There is a woman standing on the shore, looking out to
sea. She is waiting for her lover to return and he never comes.
   Why did he leave, why did she not go with him?
   Was he a fisherman, was he lost?
   Or is she waiting for him to come back?
   Too late to long for a lover after you have sent him away.
   They cross the seas and they drown or they disappear.

Sixty-seven

Outside the window, the Marne is frozen, the night black. A single tail light moves along the road from Reims. We snuggle under thick coverlets. Her thigh is draped across mine.

— You woke me sexually and emotionally, she whispers to me in the dark.

It is the most wonderful thing any woman could say to a man.

But instead she looks tearful, edgy. You sense remorse and guilt. The blue eyes are liquid.

— That's a bad thing because . . .?

— I wish you hadn't sometimes. It makes it harder for me with Paul.

Her take on this leaves me stunned. It seems that finding her sexuality and an emotional life has made her life with Paul harder to reconstruct.

I have a text message stored on my cell phone, still, after

fifteen months: *You have woken me and stirred emotions and desire that I thought only happened in fairy tales.*

Next morning her face is drawn with guilt. I long for a moment when champagne might mean celebration and laughter and not refuge, when the dull ache behind my eyes might be from the wine the night before and not the impossible dilemmas of living.

Paul and Susan do not drink.

We walk along the frozen banks of the river, find a foozball game in the local café. It makes her laugh again, or pretend to. I can never tell which.

– Thank you for loving me, she whispers.

It does not occur to me to say it back to her, not then. It feels good, being her benefactor. I don't see how this stands between us.

– You said to me once that I made you see love in colour. Did you mean that?

– A part of me did.

This is how it is with Anna. She says things a man longs to hear from a woman, and then takes them away again. Everything shifts, nothing is solid. You cannot trust anything she says to take your weight.

I watch her run giggling down the frozen cobblestones in the aptly named Bouzy, between champagne houses – quick, before they shut! – free and crazy and guiltless, Anna as I love her most, with her wonderful elfin grin, playful and skittish and holding on to my arm.

A week later she is back in London, and I am in Hanford, staring at a flickering computer screen, still unable to write.

I speak to David perhaps once or twice a week on the phone. He answers in monosyllables my solicitous questions about his wellbeing and hangs up at the first opportunity.

There is nothing to be done but wait and see if he will come back.

Sixty-eight

Sue's journals have shown me a side of her I have never seen before.

> *You know I'm talking to Mark again, really talking and he is being so considerate and loving. Why then do I feel so angry and so tired? Really nothing has changed – he and I have grown apart and then we have moments that recapture what we once valued but we can't sustain it perhaps because so much has occurred between those moments. I feel myself back on that same merry-go-round . . .*

I never knew she felt this way and this was just six months before we parted. I thought I was the one that was unhappy.

There is peace and consolation here. It was not just me. There is a profound sense of relief in hearing these things from her, even now.

I remember her saying many times that whenever she tried to talk to me my eyes glazed over. But for years I held on to her, did whatever was necessary to keep the marriage together.

Wasn't this what I wanted, for her to talk to me like this? Wasn't this what she wanted, for me to listen to her as avidly as I read her journals, the way I listen to Anna?

Well, I thought so, then; it seems to me now that what I really wanted was her vindication, her imprimatur on my decision to leave, and the journals have finally given me this.

She comes in the night, her ghost, gliding into my dreams. I am in a church and she is wearing white and I am about to get married. Even in the dream there is a sudden feeling of panic.

I am a groom who has showed up in the wrong church. I know I am marrying the wrong woman and I flee past the startled guests and run panicked and sweating to Anna's apartment.

She is not there.

But the next day, while I am still disturbed and perturbed by my dreams, Anna calls: she has to go to New York and San Francisco for work. Will I meet her there?

I desperately want to, but stall for time. I have to stop this. I can't.

Mark D'Arbanville

Sixty-nine

An email from Anna:

I can smell his skin
His arm is around my hip
Reassuring and protective
I can feel him watching me as I cross the room
He has amazing eyes that seem so deep and blue that
I can jump in and seek refuge
He speaks a melody of wonderful things to me
On occasions I do hear and feel exhilarated
I can cry and know that he will listen
I can disappoint him and know that he will
forgive me
I can amaze and bewilder him and yet he does not
tire of me
I can see parts of him he didn't know anyone
could see

I can help him see the beauty in him like he does
for me
I can see his talents, his passion, his love of life and
his intense love for others
He is my best friend and no woman could ever ask
for any more

I decide to go to New York.

Mark D'Arbanville

Seventy

Early March but numbing cold outside, dry and bitter. The hotel window looks out over an empty basketball court, glazed with ice, twelve storeys below. The brown towers of Manhattan, desolate and silent, like life after she is gone. The night closes around us.

We are huddled in our New York hotel, below the iron looming of the Queensboro bridge. She has never seen a porn movie so I skip through the TV menu and buy one. She is disappointed. Great sex happens in the head and heart; pornography is just naked bodies moving into different positions.

I turn it off after fifteen minutes. Instead she ties me naked to a chair beside the dresser. Then she lies on the bed and slowly takes off her clothes, rubbing oil into her breasts. She lies face down on the bed and brings herself to a climax while I watch.

It is the most intimate and erotic moment I have ever had with a woman: I have not touched her and I have not come.

When she finishes she puts her face in the crook of her arm and watches me with huge blue eyes and I am in her thrall.

What has happened to me? Before Anna I never saw another woman as intimately as this, could not make love for hours and hours, always shut my eyes to private fantasy as I came.

Later we both lie naked on sweat-damp sheets. I stare at the red digital numbers on the bedside clock, time slipping away, stolen moments always.

There have been too many hotel rooms. I want to emerge from the shadows, the hero – or more likely the villain – from the pages of this novel, want to be real, even though I may be unforgiven and unredeemed.

Mark D'Arbanville

Seventy-one

What I want.

To drink a bottle of champagne with her in a bar and chase it with Cocksucking Cowboys. To hear every dirty story she's ever imagined. To send roses to her office. To hear her dreams, her fears and her secrets. To hold her coat for her. To lie between her legs, watch her face as I tease her with my tongue and hold her hands as she comes. To buy her French perfume. The thrill of seeing her in a black dress. To watch her put on her make-up in her underwear. To softly kiss her face. To laugh at her jokes. To see her smile. To curl into her in bed. To listen to her talk about the latest book she's read. To listen to the sound of her voice, torchy and elegant with the lilt of a laugh in it. To kiss her and feel her snake hips press into me. To talk with her for hours about books, about life, about people. To slip my fingers between her legs and find her already wet. To tease her about her reverse angle parking. To play foozball with her. To open the car door for her. To make her feel like the most beautiful woman in the world. To hold out her chair for her when she sits down. To meet her eyes across a room and both know what each other is thinking. To slow dance with her.

Text messages.

Mark D'Arbanville

Seventy-two

On the flight between New York and San Francisco we talk frankly for the first time about our affair.

– Would you have done this if you knew where it would end? she asks me.

How can I answer this? There was never any choice. I was drawn to her. I simply found her irresistible, and still do.

– I thought we could have our own private world, she murmurs, staring out of the window at the northern star.

As insane as it now seems, this is what I thought also, at the beginning, that I would learn something from her, take this lesson back to my marriage and be a better man for it.

She is drinking her Veuve Clicquot too fast.

– I just thought it would be an amazing affair that would turn into an incredible lifelong friendship, she says.

And really, that's the heart of the problem for us both. An amazing affair followed by an incredible lifelong friendship is how couples with a happy fifty year marriage describe their lives together.

An affair is just about sex, danger and making a wife or husband pay more attention. But this affair wouldn't end when it was supposed to, it refused to stay inside the lines.

– Do you have any regrets? she asks me. About Susan?

– I never loved Susan. Not really.

Perhaps I want to convince myself, or convince Anna. If that is my intention, I don't get the reaction I want.

– I cannot believe the man I know could live with a woman for so long and not love her.

– It was different with Susan.

But I can't retreat. Anna looks pinched and cynical. Alcohol lightens her moods or plunges her into dark places, and I can never predict which way she will go.

I think about what she has said. I listen to the muted and tinny clash of music from the headphones on my lap, the high pitched background whine of the 737 engines. Others are asleep around us, among the midnight debris of blankets and newspapers and magazines, a spilled wine glass rolls under the seat in front.

I did love Susan once, I murmur. It was supposed to be until death do us part. But I changed and so did she. It's not supposed to be the way it is, but it's the way it works.

I turn around. Anna is asleep, curled into her seat.

Sleepless, I think about my life with Susan. I realise the man Anna knows is not the man Susan knew. I suspect that I know a much different Anna than the one Paul knows, mine perhaps unrecognisable to him. Her father, her mother, her sisters would probably be shocked and disbelieving.

I wonder which is the real one. I know this incarnation, the

Mark D'Arbanille

way I am now, feels right for me. She will have to make her own choice, or perhaps she will make no choice at all, live this double life, like I did, for a decade yet.

Our short time together in this surreal world of hotels and airport business lounges is gone too soon. On our last night together I manufacture a fight in the hotel room, unable to contain my grief at leaving her again. And so I find myself walking along the perpendicular streets of San Francisco. Alcatraz looms in the darkness of the bay, laughing gangs of men sprawl from a bar. I stand on Fisherman's Wharf consumed by a terrible rage at the gods.

My fulling heart needs a place to rest and instead I am lost with a woman who once called me the most special man in the world right after she told me she did not love me enough.

There is nothing here I can understand.

Seventy-three

There have been too many goodbyes.

We said goodbye for ever one early morning in a car in Hyde Park but in May I met her in our hideaway cottage in Lincolnshire and slow danced next to the cold fireplace while outside crows drew together in the mist.

We said goodbye again for ever after Susan died but the quickening of the New Year found us walking hand in hand across snow covered cobblestones in the Marne.

Too many goodbyes and it seems to me they go more easily for her, for there is a part of her that wants me gone, a relief from the guilt perhaps. She returns from the adventure with her prize, with a memory to carry into the future as sustenance, a future she calls black and uncertain.

I always wonder which goodbye will be the last.

We are in the day room of a San Francisco airport hotel. It is empty, still early morning, stark and bright, the crisp newspapers unread and through the windows there is a view of the

Mark D'Arbanville

control towers at the international airport to remind us that this is a place of leaving.

I have to go home; her business partner is joining her here and Anna trusts no one with her secrets.

We go into the bathroom and shower together. I stand behind her, her fists beating the glass as we make love. Then she throws towels on the cold tiles and guides me on top of her and inside her and as I come we are both crying.

– Never say never, she whispers.

We dress, shivering.

– This is your choice, I shout angrily as we embrace before we go outside for her taxi. You just love him more than you love me.

– It's not a competition, she says. You can't compare one person to another.

– How else do you decide who you will be with?

I have compared her with other women, just as beautiful and smart, but with whom I felt nothing at all.

– I love you both. It's just different. I love him in a different way.

What has love got to do with this? If she loves him so fucking much, why isn't she happy?

She leaves me at the airport and goes back to her other life, her real life. She cannot do this again until she is sorted, she tells me.

I think sometimes that I would be perfect for her if I were just a fantasy, hidden in a locker at the airport. Then she could retreat to the affair whenever she needed to, and not have to worry about hurting me, or hurting Paul.

the Naked Husband

But what good is a real life if you need refuge from it? Isn't that why I left my own marriage behind?

As she drives away in the taxi I feel a piece of me die. I love her too much, as she said. I have lost any instinct for survival.

Mark D'Arbanille

Seventy-four

– **Of course, as soon as** she chooses one of you, or chooses anyone really, she's out of control, Jen says. She can't let go but she doesn't want to hold on. The proverbial tiger by the balls.

She is delighted, of course, how delicious this situation is for the casual observer.

She pours coffee into two mugs.

We are in her studio, which is hidden away among creepers and a rambling blackberry at the end of the garden. The house, a big mock Tudor detached two storey, was bought with her husband's dosh. He's a solicitor, specialising in divorces; he's also a season ticket holder at Manchester United but is often too busy to go, which means he has a lot more friends than he otherwise would.

– If she commits, what's going to happen? Jen says. She'll have to come through for someone.

– I don't think that's it, Jen.

I take my coffee and go back to the table, flick through

the treatment she has printed out. It's a script on infidelity we are both working on and Anna is interested in optioning it. Another of life's ironies.

At least I am back working again. After eighteen months, it's a relief.

– Right now she has you both where she wants you.

– I don't want to talk about this anymore.

– You both want her. So she only has to threaten to leave one of you and she's back in control.

– In control of what? In control of her own uncertainty and unhappiness?

Jen makes a face.

– Of course. Isn't that what we all dream about?

She sits down, tendrils of steam rising from her coffee mug. It is cold in here this morning, frost on the windowpanes, outside the world is still and brown, laced with white.

– You know what they say. Treat 'em mean to keep 'em keen.

I am familiar with the expression, even heard Anna use it once. It's exhausting, these tactics of love and loving can drain you and leave you as paranoid and isolated as an airman downed over enemy desert.

– If there's no challenge, will you both still love her? Perhaps that's the way she's always played the game, or it's always how the game's been played with her.

– You're fucking cynical, Jen.

– I'm a fucking realist, Mark.

– Let's talk about the script.

– I don't know about you, but every time I had an affair it's made Terry try harder.

– What does that say about your relationship with Terry?

– That it's normal?

– That it's fucked.

– That's good coming from you, the expert in human relationships.

I look out of the window and sulk a little.

– There's always a lovor and a lovee, you know, she says.

– A what?

– Someone does the chasing, the other one hangs off, the one with the power. Only power's addictive, and so then the lovee can't let go either. It feels good, rescuing someone, being adored and needed. It's heady stuff. Look at you and Sue.

– Crap, I sneer, shaking my head, but she's right on the money.

I loved Sue's addiction to me, no one else in the world depended on me like she did, and it meant I didn't have to depend on myself, didn't even have to like myself. I thought I was in control but the truth was I didn't have the balls to let go and be powerless with someone else. Until Anna. And even then I hesitated for months.

I have seen what love is like from both sides, I have now been both lovor and lovee. Never got me anywhere either way.

There has to be some way for men and women, without lovors and lovees. Does it always have to be a battle to get the upper hand? Can there be some place of trust and intimacy without any hand at all?

Jen is smiling, knowing she has found my emotional G-spot. She is so smug, I hate her sometimes.

The Naked Husband

– You and Terry . . . are you the lovor or the lovee?

– I used to be the lovee. When women get over forty they become lovors. It's Terry's turn now.

– How do you feel about that?

Jen sips her coffee.

– Are you going to talk all morning or are we going to get this script finished?

There is a crow sitting on the bare branches of the apple tree outside the window. It caws plaintively to a pale and empty sky.

Mark D'Arbanille

Seventy-five

On her birthday Anna has been walking by the Thames for hours, confused and upset over her life and where it is taking her. She calls me on her cell phone and pours out her heart. She consoles herself at the end, as she often does, by telling me that her life is not so bad, that she really has nothing to complain of, that others have had much worse lives.

After each outpouring she busies herself with her life again, with work, with family, and this gnawing pain is sidelined until the next birthday, the next family christening or wedding or funeral, the next Valentine's Day, when the sense of time passing is impossible to ignore and the pain spills out of her again.

Which is why this birthday finds her walking alone on the London Embankment delaying the moment when she must go back to her life, to be good again for others, wholesome but not whole.

Seventy-six

Dear Mark,

*I am really worried about you and the effect I have
on you, it has been really bothering me all week.*

*I hate how you feel about Paul and I understand
you have every right but I am just hurting you more.
I am going into a dark place again where I hate
everything and everyone. I don't know if I will ever
change my situation, I just don't know. As you told
me before I don't know if I know how to be in love
really, I mix everything up, my mood changes,
I swing from one emotion to another.*

*The past is like a furnace burning in my soul that
shows its head in so many ugly ways as a feeling and
sometimes as a vision and my heart starts to race or
just an incredible sadness sweeps over me. I have
burdened you with something that is really too much*

Mark D'Arbanville

for anyone to try and have to deal with and you try
so very hard to understand.

I am in my worried mode at the moment, really
bad, I am scared for you, and for me, really scared.
I just don't know if I can offer you a future or not,
and by now this should be sorted, this is absolutely
not acceptable to be doing to you or letting yourself
be involved this way.

Today is not a great day for me, everything
is grey.

Anna xx

Seventy-seven

A restaurant in Chelsea. She says she is interested in my script. It is an excuse to see each other, and we take it.

The straw glow of wine, amber candlelight. She leans forward, décolletage highlighted by the fold of her arms. Deliberately. The waiter has brought desserts and she slips a cherry from her plate into her mouth and holds it firmly between her teeth, and pops out the stalk.

She grins and rolls the cherry around her tongue, lips a little apart, wet with gloss. Her bedroom eyes speculate and drop to my groin. I hold my breath, watch the small red fruit as she rolls it around her pink and moist tongue.

Suddenly she chokes on the pit and cherry juice is sprayed across the white linen tablecloth in an explosion of coughing. She barks like a seal. The sound interrupts whispered and intimate conversations around the room and heads turn in our direction. Laughing, I lean across the table and pat her on the back.

Mark D'Arbanville

She gets her breath, and gulps a glass of water brought to her by a solicitous waiter. My sex siren, I say to her. My sex goddess and utter goof-off. She starts to giggle and cough at once. I feel my heart swell.

– I adore you, I say in the car on the way home from the restaurant. I absolutely adore you.

But now, suddenly, her mood is changed.

– You shouldn't love me, she says. I'm like poison for you.

What can you say to someone you love when they tell you not to love them? It is like she is physically pushing me in the chest, away from her. Once she asked me not to hate her; now she actively encourages me to it.

– I'd rather be anyone but me, she says.

– I don't know how you can say that.

– If someone doesn't like themselves, it doesn't help you telling them how wonderful they are. Just the opposite.

This amazing woman, adorable in white blouse and black knee-length skirt, rose tinted glasses and hair in tortoiseshell comb, to die for.

– You just want to hurt people, push them away so they'll scream at you, tell you you're shit. Then you can say, see, I was right all along.

– If you know that, why do you let it happen?

– Because I'd rather be anyone but me, she says and we ride the rest of the way to her apartment in silence.

Seventy-eight

A pattern emerging. She withdraws when I pressure her to leave him, I get frustrated with her, so I do not call, and she does not call, and it seems it is over. But being apart is too painful so I call her and tell her, tell myself, that it doesn't matter about Paul, that I can just be her friend.

But talking to her on the phone leads to intimacy and intimacy leads to desire and this ends inevitably in another secret rendezvous. And the most natural thing when we are talking so much and making love so passionately is to long for a real relationship. But with Anna there is always a wall beyond which I cannot pass, and when I try to break through and demand more than this, she withdraws and so the cycle begins again.

With Sue I had history, friendship and familiarity. What I found with Anna was passion, fun and the sharing of our creativity.

With both women, sooner or later, I felt locked out. In the

Mark D'Arbanville

end Sue and Anna withdrew, like a shell closing over a pearl. The treasure may be different, but the defences are exactly the same.

— She'll go to counselling next, Jen says. We have finished the script and now we have settled into the snug at the Wheatsheaf to celebrate and drink too much, again.

— Crap.

— She will. Watch.

But she's right. Anna has already started counselling with Paul, but I don't tell Jen that, don't give her the satisfaction.

I went to marriage counselling with Sue years ago, hoping the shrink would get me off the hook, make the hard decisions for me. I wanted him to tell us it was time to part and I would be vindicated.

We made him umpire but he called it a draw and sent us away to sort out the winners and losers ourselves. And we couldn't.

— You have to work at a marriage, Mark.

— Like hard labour?

— You know what I mean.

— When do you stop? Do you just keep going till you're too exhausted to stand up? Or until one of you kills themselves?

That was uncalled for. But if anything, that's what I really blame myself for; pushing Sue too far. Jen shakes her head and downs her third vodka.

— Could you have saved your marriage to Sue?

It is a question I have asked myself many times. People ask this as if a marriage is a life: could you have saved Sue from drowning if you had learned to swim? But a marriage is not a life, it is not sacrosanct. Friends and family looked at us both as if it was a calamity, and looked for ways to repair something that was irreparable, and when it was done they looked for someone to blame.

Some relationships last a lifetime but some do not; and people do change, even good people, good fathers and wives, good sons and daughters. I woke one day to find Sue was a war I no longer needed to wage.

— We were like oysters, Jen. We clung on to each other's rock because we were just too fucking frightened to let go.

— It must have been good once.

— It was. But we changed. At least, I know I did. I tried to make her change with me and that wasn't fair. My only other choice was to go back to the way I was to make the marriage work.

Just like you, I want to say.

— When you love someone, how can you leave them? she says, and you know she is certainly talking about her own marriage now.

— Sue told me I should love her unconditionally. But I don't know that we can, not inside a marriage. A relationship is the most conditional thing there is. I love my mother unconditionally, I love David unconditionally. But I don't have to live with them every day. I don't have to make love to them. Why am I living with someone if they don't enrich my life, make it better?

Jen downs her vodka. She pushes her glass across the table.

— I'll have another one, she says, and by now she is slurring her words.

Mark D'Arbanille

– Don't you need to be getting home?

She lights a cigarette. She has recently taken up smoking again.

– To fucking Terry? No thanks.

Seventy-nine

There is a circadian rhythm to the affair; we say goodbye at an airport or a train station somewhere, and for a
few weeks she is cool with me on the telephone, her voice
echoes on the long distance line. She is going to sort out
her life.

But then some need in her I cannot fathom brings her
back. We arrange to meet and she is excited and eager, but as
the rendezvous draws closer the guilt bites again. For the first
few days together everything else is forgotten; I am the secret
addiction she hides from the world, the shame and the habit
she promises herself she will kick. Afterwards, she vows this is
definitely the last time, she must sort out her life, and the cycle
begins again.

I recognise the trap she is in, for I spent years on this same
treadmill of longing and guilt. Now, in a different role, I tell
myself that I will save her somehow, that in her damage lies
my chance to be loved, because then I will understand why

198   *Mark D'Arbanville*

she loves me and I will have some control over this. Needing is something I can understand, I seek out damage in women like a dog sniffing fear. If I am not caretaking I simply do not know what to do.

– I'm so blessed to have a friend like you, she said to me once, I hope we will always be a part of each other's lives.

As if some foul-tempered Greek god has somehow already decreed against it.

Her sense of hopelessness and futility is enervating. It is as if she thinks she has no choice.

– Why the hell are you still with this guy? You don't love him, Anna.

Listen to me. I have become a monster, a stranger to myself. I'm like every other man in her life, telling her what to do and what to think.

– Maybe it's not perfect. Who said it had to be all or nothing?

– How many times have I heard you say, there has to be more? Why don't you just get on with things, for God's sake?

This is about control now. Whether it is done with smiles or with silence or, as some men do, with violence, control is the mathematics of loving.

But instead of needing me, as Susan had, Anna retreats. Suddenly I have no control at all. I am lost in this new role, belly up and exposed. I have no idea what to do. Now I wonder if it is better to be numb or to be hurt.

– I cannot take any more of your pain, she whispers one night. I cannot endure any more of this guilt about cheating on Paul, and for causing you this pain.

– You are not responsible for anything, Anna. I never said you were.

Or did I? It is how we all cling to love, after all. I am no longer sure what I have said to her, or what she has heard.

Einstein once said that if you have one hand on a hot plate and one hand in a freezer, on average you will be comfortable. This is what we do in love, I suppose. Once you have been really burned, you put your hand in the freezer, so that you don't get scalded. It seems the reasonable thing to do.

Mark D'Arbanville

Eighty

Eighteen months after the funeral, Sue's ashes are still in the hard grey plastic container I got from the funeral home. I cannot bear to touch them, I am still so angry.

But one night, cold and desperate and tired, I take them to bed and curl around them in a ball and the grief chokes out of me, I can hardly breathe, and when I am done, I try to warm her, as I used to, curling my body around the grey box to warm the ashes inside and I tell her she is going to be all right.

I am dying because the way I have lived for the last forty years is not working anymore . . . I have to trust and listen to the voice inside. I know I'll continue to die inside and begin to die outside if I don't do this.

Oh God, I whisper to the empty dark, I am so sorry.

It started out a fairy tale romance. Only the prince and the princess did not live happily ever after. His suit of armour grew rusty and she traded her golden tresses for a hairstyle that was a little more practical. We tell ourselves that this is just the way love is. But maybe we tell ourselves wrong.

I did not want her to bend herself out of shape for me. I wanted her to be herself.

I know we could have worked out a compromise, but I didn't want my marriage and my life to be a compromise. I would have died inside and outside too.

I toss and turn in a disturbed half-sleep and then jerk suddenly awake and Susan is sitting on the end of the bed.

– Susan?

– You don't have to do this anymore, Mark.

– I'm sorry. I'm so sorry.

– It's the past, she tells me. Leave it behind. Let me go.

I loved her once, lovde her more than I could say or was willing to admit. What happened to it? How do two people turn joy into chains?

– I feel like we failed.

– We had some beautiful years, and a beautiful son. It was just time to finish. Everything finishes, one way or another. I should have left you years ago.

– Back then I wouldn't have let you go.

We think we know what love is, but we don't. We come together as lovers for the laughter and the passion, and over time we turn it into duty and care. And then one day you find it again, and like a starving man at a banquet, you reach again for that which is lost. Only by then it is too late to go forward, and too late to go back.

– I'm leaving now, she whispers.

Mark D'Arbanille

– Susan?

– It's going to be all right now, Mark. It's going to be all right.

She slips under sleep's dark and forbidding gate. I wake in the morning, not sure if it was just a dream or I am going crazy. Susan and I have nothing more to say to each other in this life; but I want her voice to be heard before I let her go for the last time.

Eighty-one

Outside the world is swathed in frost, hard bitten and brown. The brick outhouse and tumbledown shed in the garden are remnants from another time; inside, the Lincolnshire cottage has been renovated with the accoutrements of the modern world, central heating and double glazing. We are cocooned in a superheated world, lying together, nuzzling in the spa, frosted glass shutting out the grey of English winter.

The room is lit with candles. She lies against my chest, with her back to me and I massage her soapy breasts and then my fingers explore her as she strains against me. She comes suddenly with her face half turned towards me, her mouth hot and wet and her tiny cries bringing me to the edge.

Afterwards she lies back on the other side of the tub, grinning, but her hair catches alight on one of the candles. My sweetheart. My siren. My goof-off.

We have the trappings of intimacy without its substance. I can close my eyes and picture every part of her naked, even

Mark D'Arbanville

when she is far away, she has shared her body's climax and release so many times, I have looked into the blue well of her eyes as I have come inside her, but her heart I still cannot see into. It is a secret garden with many locked doors behind the overgrown walls.

What does she really want? I know she wants this, today, or she would not be here. Beyond that, I do not know. Paul's shadow obscures everything.

She calls me her lover and best friend, and I wonder if there can be more than this between a man and woman. I ask her what else she wants from her partner in this life but she will not answer.

— I don't understand why you're doing this! If you love him so much that you can't leave, why are you here with me?

She does not answer, her face changes, becomes that of a little girl.

— Is it because he was in your life first? Is that what it's about? Chronology?

She wilts in the face of my rage. This is primal. I feel it building from the inside, taking over. She does not answer me, retreats into silence.

I am angry at her for putting the three of us through this, angry for all the wives and mistresses and husbands and lovers through all time who have waited in vain, angry at her for finding so many reasons to stay when she gave me all the reasons she wanted to leave.

All I want is for her to tell me why she stays, tell me how she loves Paul in ways she could never possibly love me, so I can walk away in peace and leave her behind.

What is she doing? I wonder. Is she punishing Paul? What does she want from him now? She long ago had him begging, he will do whatever she wants now. What else does she hope to squeeze out of him? She will destroy him if she does not take him as he is or let him go.

– If you don't want me, why do you keep loving me?

– I love you both, she says.

– That's not the point! I loved Susan. I still do. But I didn't want to live with her anymore.

– Don't yell at me.

– You have hurt me more than I ever thought any woman could hurt me! For months you told me how much was missing from your life and now you say you love him and you don't want to give him up. From the very beginning you gave me one reason after another why we couldn't be together and as I knocked them down you came up with another one! Is there any way you can think of to torture me further?

– You said to me once we could help each other without disrupting each other's lives.

– Well, that was pretty naive, wasn't it?

– You promised.

– All that did was help us maintain these shallow relationships we had in our lives. We were frauds, both of us! We were lying to everyone!

– Stop it, Mark.

– Every day you change your fucking mind! One day you're going to leave and sort yourself out, the next day you love him. Why? You can't or won't explain. Move in with me then. No. Why? Again, you can't or you won't tell me. This is so fucking

Mark D'Arbanville

unfair. Did you mean anything you ever said to me? Was anything you said real? For God's sake, go back to Paul, if that's what you want. You've cheated on me as well as on him! The further I went for you, the further you retreated. You must be saying one thing to me and another to him. You were happy with me as long as I didn't get too close. I don't think you want anyone to get too close to you. That's why Paul fits you like a fucking glove!

I am panting. Rage has taken my breath away. I get out of the spa and dress quickly. I get in the car and drive too fast through the back lanes, past twisted trees and bitter-eyed crows, twice skidding on black ice, not caring, the winter fields either side of the road as hard and frostbitten as my heart.

When I get back she is waiting for me outside, wrapped in her coat and scarf against the cold she hates so much, forlorn.

– What do you want from me? I shout at her. What the hell do you want?

– I want you to hold me, she murmurs.

And with that, I come undone.

And so I hold her, feel her warmth through our coats, her cold nose nuzzles wet against my neck. I cannot hold her any closer but I cannot get close at all.

Eighty-two

I am seven years old and I have come home early from school and my mother is leaning against the wall in the kitchen with her face in the crook of her arm. Her shoulders are gently shaking and I know she is crying. I hug her skirts.

– What's wrong, Mum? What's wrong?

I feel her stiffen, aware of my presence.

She pushes me away and wipes her face with her apron. Suddenly she is smiling, and the world has gone crazy.

– Nothing's wrong, dear. I was just peeling onions.

It doesn't make sense. But I accept her lie because even at seven I have learned that this is what I must do to survive this family; if I pretend to be happy I am rewarded, if I am sad and disruptive I am punished.

I do not remember when I decided it was my job to save her, but the saving of her was where my rage was born. For to love, I learned, you must not want anything for yourself. Love is responsibility.

Mark D'Arbanville

Love is rescuing a woman who would die without you.

On another day later in time she is again leaning against the wall in the kitchen with her face in the crook of her arm. Her shoulders are gently shaking and I know she is crying. But this time I do not hug her skirts for I tower over her now, a man, and this terrible coldness I once knew as guilt has turned into a flaming ball of rage.

– What the hell is wrong?

– You know what's wrong.

I clench my fists in frustration and the woman in the kitchen turns to face me. It is Susan.

The rage of the child has become the marriage of the man. I want to walk out of the door and never come back. I cannot walk out of the door because it is my job to stay here and keep her from whatever disaster will befall her without me. She is a good woman and she relies on me for her happiness, this Ivy, this Sue. This is how I have come to measure myself, this is the measure of me as a good son, a good husband, a good man.

– Is this because I went away fishing for the weekend?

– And left me to sort out the problem with David.

– David's fine. You didn't need me here.

– I think he's taking drugs!

– He's smoking grass. A lot of the kids are. It could have waited. Is this why you haven't been speaking to me since I got home?

– Do the crime, you do the time.

– Christ, this is a marriage not a penal colony. I didn't even know what you were mad about.

I take Susan by the shoulders.

– I cannot read your fucking mind! I cannot know what is going on in your head unless you fucking tell me! How can I possibly know unless you say something?

And then from nowhere I hear myself shouting at her.

– You don't have to be angry at me! I'm not your father! I am not the one you're mad at!

I stare at the frightened woman in my arms. It is Anna.

Mark D'Arbanville

Eighty-three

The places we have made love.

A hideaway cottage on the Irish Sea, licking melted chocolate from each other and afterwards she slept coiled in my arms, her hair tickling my face.

The shower in the day room at a San Francisco airport hotel, on the cold tile floors, when I thought we would never see each other again.

The carpet of a friend's apartment when we fell off the bed and I almost knocked myself out on the bedside table.

Drunk once, in a room in an *auberge* in France, when we both were so exhausted we fell asleep in each other's arms, joined together.

In a cove on a beach, a towel wrapped around her while my fingers explored her and two men swam in the shallows. I whispered to her a favourite fantasy and she bit my hand until it bruised to keep from crying out.

The sauna in a major city hotel, while I kept watch for other guests through the glass in the wooden door.

She promised to take me higher than I'd ever been and kept her promise. But now I'm stranded, beyond the tide line.

Our most recent separation has lasted two months, but now we are drawn back together again, like twins, being apart too painful to bear.

Mark D'Arbanville

Eighty-four

Another London hotel, anonymous and plush and bleak. There are narrow carpeted corridors with framed prints of fox hunts, superheated rooms and thick quilts on the beds.

There is a knock on the door. I open it. The woman is in her thirties, attractive, with glossy long black hair. I am just out of the shower, just a towel wrapped around my waist, and I am aware of my own vulnerability.

She looks me up and down.

– You rang down for a massage? she says, her accent thick, Eastern European.

– Come in.

She tells me to lie face down on the bed. I take off the towel and do as she asks. She kneels on the bed. Her perfume overwhelms me and I feel myself quickly aroused. She has a small black leather pouch and from it, out of the corner of my eye, I see her take a small plastic bottle of lotion.

She kneels astride my back. I feel the heat of her as she starts to massage my shoulders.

– What is your name?

– Anastasia.

– It's a pretty name. Where are you from?

– From Russia.

– You're a very attractive woman. You must hear that all the time.

– Thank you, she says. She seems melancholy, intense. Her hands move down my body, start to massage my thighs. A hand slips for a moment between my legs and I gasp.

– Does your boyfriend know what you do for a living?

– He knows.

– And he doesn't mind?

She does not answer. She leans forward and her hair brushes my cheek.

– They said downstairs that you wanted special massage, she whispers.

I roll over and she smiles when she sees the effect she has had on me. She slips her dress over her head. She is wearing a black bra and G-string and is utterly beautiful. I am aching for her. She spills more of the lotion onto the head of my engorged penis.

And then.

– Christ!

I scream and roll off the bed, lie curled up on the thick-carpeted floor with tears of pain running down my face, both hands cupping my groin.

– For God's sake! . . . What's in that . . . fucking stuff?

Anna stares at me horrified and bewildered by what has happened.

Mark D'Arbanville

– It's just hand lotion.

I reach for the bottle. I read the ingredients, squinting against the pain.

– It's got menthol in it, you ditz!

She does not know whether to laugh or run and fetch a doctor.

– Shall I get water?

– Get a fucking firehose!

It feels as if someone has poured napalm into my urethra. Her face makes me laugh in between spasms of pain; stricken, comical, appalled. I grab her with one free hand and hug her to my shoulder. Anna, in her role as mysterious Russian hotel masseuse, has fucked up.

– Are you all right?

– I don't know!

– I'm sorry!

And then we both start to laugh again.

Later, lying on the bed, she kneels astride me and looks for any lasting damage.

– Why won't he get big? He always gets big if I do this.

– You've scared him.

– Won't he come out to play with me anymore?

– Oh, I don't think things are that bad.

She wiggles my penis from side to side and puts on a comic voice.

– Gosh, they're funny things when they're small, she says.

Something else I love about her. The clown and the sex goddess. She captivates me utterly. Nothing compares.

– He's not a glove puppet, for Christ's sake.

Later we watch television together. Her hair is a mess, my bewitching Russian masseuse tucked up in her pyjamas in the crook of my arm, utterly adorable.

– I want to watch my crime program, she says, and fumbles with the remote.

– There, I say, finding the channel.

– Let me watch this and then I'm yours, she mumbles, and ten minutes later she is snoring softly into the pillow, her glasses askew.

That something so ordinary and so normal should mean so much to me.

Once I was loved for being a husband; for my dependability, my reliability, my ordinariness. Now I am cast as lover, the adventure, the excitement, the dirty secret. And I resent it just as much.

I want to be both to one woman and it's what all men, perhaps all naked husbands, want more than anything.

The next day she gets an early morning flight for a business meeting in the States. I go with her to the airport, plan to get the express back to Paddington and a train to Manchester.

I turn away from her at the airport lounge, do not want another tearful parting. But after she has passed through security I go back and watch her through the window. I tap on the glass, mouthing 'I love you' and performing a little pantomime, pointing to myself, then my heart and then to her. But she is facing away from me, watching CNN on the wall-mounted television. Other passengers see me though, and stare at me as if I am crazy. I try and get her attention by calling her on her cell phone, but it is switched off.

Mark D'Arbanville

It seems like a cameo of our whole affair; I am clumsy and late and unable to get my message to her through an invisible barrier I cannot penetrate; she is facing the other way, distracted by her own private world.

She remains untouchable, a vision seen but going away, entirely out of reach.

Eighty-five

Anna sends a card:

You create a painting that leads to another world
with your words
Your eyes are like a sea of emotions that I get lost in
Your touch is as soft as a feather
And your embrace as warm as the strongest fire
Your voice is full of passion and your heart is full
of love
For anybody who meets you
They see colour, the colour of your love

Mark D'Arbanille

Eighty-six

– **She's never going to leave him,** Jen says with barely concealed delight. She tried to warn you, and you didn't listen. She gave you enough hints.

This is the part that galls me the most, the satisfaction people take in my predicament. It is as if it confirms their worst suspicions about love and about human nature, better to compromise than risk everything for the one that really stops your heart.

– He loves her more than she loves him, now. They've swapped places. He's the lovor and she's the lovee and she's in control. Why would she give that up? It's safe.

Jen is right, she did try to warn me, many times. It's me that won't let go. I'm the fool here.

I try and imagine myself as Anna, waiting for Paul to love her all these years, and now he is on his knees, saying he will do whatever it takes to get her back. I wonder what I would do, if I would take what I had worked so hard to have, relish the intoxicating power of it. But power in itself is a trap, for you have to work so hard to keep it. It was the story of my own marriage, constantly crushing minor rebellions among a dissatisfied and surly electorate.

– You don't fit the perfect picture, sport. You've been married, you've got baggage and a teenage son. What's her family going to say? She has to make it work with him. She plays by their rules and they won't accept you. He's single, the family likes him. You've got no show.

Jen dumps down another mocha with cream. She's put on a few pounds since she's been counselling me like this.

– Sorry, she says, seeing the pained expression on my face. I'm just an old truth teller.

Somehow the truth, if that is what it is, has brightened her day. I know what she is thinking: nobody is ever really happy. Everything fucks up somehow. If someone ever finds the way to the holy grail and a happy marriage, she might have to go back to the coalface and do something about her and Terry.

And there I am, the lovor seeing love from the other side, the torturer laid out on his own rack. I imagine Sue in my position, loving me all those years, waiting for me to love her back.

Every wheel turns.

Susan must take some grim satisfaction in this, I think, but that is unfair. Knowing her as I do, I imagine it is more likely that today, whatever heaven she is in, she wants only that I find a resolution now, Anna too, for us all to find our way through this.

Mark D'Arbanville

Eighty-seven

David is home for the Christmas holidays and we stare at each other as strangers. He looks odd in maroon blazer and grey flannel trousers, a man dressed as a schoolboy, down on his face now, he'll be shaving soon.

His eyes are hooded and wary.

Like many parents I am bewildered and saddened and depressed by the results of my parenting. I see rage in his eyes; he does not like me.

I always thought I would be the perfect father, the perfect role model. It is not the way things have turned out. Instead he blames me for his mother's death and when we are in the same room he can barely bring himself to talk to me.

He was always my excuse for the way my life was. Unborn, he was the vital part of the perfect picture that was missing; afterwards, he became the reason not to disturb the perfect life I had built for him.

He was going to make us both perfect and successful in the

eyes of our family and our world, and later his happiness was a reason we gave to ourselves to stay together and be miserable.

I told myself I wanted him to be happy but it occurs to me now that children need to see how it is done before they can mimic it. David, I am truly afraid, may now mimic my pretence, my lies, and my failures.

— I have some things to say to you, David.

He looks disinterested.

— It's important.

I reach out and touch him on the shoulder and he flinches away. I hardly blame him. For the first fourteen years of his life I led him to believe I was perfect. So now he cannot understand why I have done this, broken up the perfect family.

— Can I go and stay with Jayden for some of the holidays? he asks. He has just walked back into the house and already he is planning his escape.

— We'll talk about it later.

— All we ever do is talk. I don't want to talk.

— Let's put your things upstairs in your bedroom first, I say, and my footsteps sound lonely in the carpeted hallway.

Eventually he follows.

Eighty-eight

The glitter of champagne in long flutes, elegant women, confident men, the premiere of a new movie. I catch a glimpse of Hugh Grant among the crowd, Simon Callow, several other luminaries of the British cinema. Anna looks across the room and catches my eye, wary of the borders of our two lives touching here tonight, there is palpable risk and she is edgy and watchful, afraid of a stray spark. Paul is in Leeds for a sales conference but her freedom is restricted by those who see her here.

Once there is a furtive touching of hands but I am on my best behaviour, and it is not until I get into the taxi to go home that I feel her finally relax. The danger of this liaison is dark and sweet as hash.

– I love you, I whisper to her late that night, sharing the same pillow.

Something dies inside each time I say those words and she does not answer. Even the most indefatigable lover becomes exhausted when his roses are left to die. I want to be good for her but all I do is summon ghosts of shame and uncertainty.

Something slips, squirming away from me.

I remember that other woman, the one who first woke the lover now prowling the room, bewildered and lost:

You have woken me and stirred emotions and desire
that I thought only happened in fairy tales.

Which one is she? Which Anna does she want to be and which is the shadow? Will she follow these emotions and desire or leave them behind, the memories and snapshots locked inside her, like a wonderful vacation she once took? If she is to resolve this and be happy, I calculate that only one Anna can survive.

I fell in love with the woman she might change into, if she chooses. The other Anna I only glimpse, the Anna she talks of but I never see, for she belongs to Paul. In turn, she sees in me the man I might one day be. But unless we both take this step forward there is no space for either of us to be together.

– I love you too, she whispers finally, and then the sting in the tail: *just not in the conventional way.*

– What the hell does that mean?

– I'm doing the best I can.

– I have no idea what you're talking about.

– You've had a conventional marriage. Did that work?

I get out of bed and prowl the living room. When I am away from her, I miss her so much. But now I leave her alone

Mark D'Arbanville

in the bedroom, to toss and turn in the bed while I pace out here in the cold.

What is wrong? Isn't this what I want, an unconventional love, the kind of love that happens even when it is not supposed to?

I hear a noise and look up. She is standing in the bedroom doorway, wearing one of my shirts.

– You see, she says. When I tell you what I think you get angry. I should leave you. I only make you unhappy.

– Please, Anna. Stop worrying about whether you make me or anyone else happy or unhappy. I just want to know what you want, what will make you happy. That's all I need to know.

– But it's true. You deserve someone who can love you properly.

Christ. It is like she has no emotional attachment to this at all. But I know this is just not true. It is like catching smoke. I want her to be human, to be a little jealous, to feel and have desire of something for herself. To get down and dirty.

As I imagine her, she is peering out from behind an impenetrable wall she has built to protect herself. I have seen glimpses of this enigmatic beauty beyond, but I cannot reach her.

– Do you have to have everything to get close?

– What do you mean by everything? Do you mean living together with no other man involved? Well then, the answer's yes. What about you? Do you really want it this way?

She does not answer.

– Anna, are you happy living like this?

The Naked Husband

– I know it's not traditional. But you had traditional and that didn't work.

– And this does? Fantasising about each other in bed and talking for hours every day on the phone while you live with another man?

– It's not you, she says, it's me.

But this is not true. My own demons have brought me here also; it is me as well, my anger and shame and guilt.

– What do you want, Anna?

– I don't know what I want. I can't even see tomorrow.

– What do you mean by that?

Her eyes become opaque.

– Sometimes I don't think I'm going to be here for very long.

She goes back to bed and leaves me standing alone in the dark. She frightens me when she says this. *I can't even see tomorrow.* It is as if she knows there may be something lurking in the future that will take her decision away.

A removalist truck perhaps.

Mark D'Arbanville

Eighty-nine

A phone call from Greg. I have avoided him in recent months. I find him too smug, too complacent.

– Hi, Mark.

– Greg. What's up?

– Need some advice. Got time for a coffee tomorrow?

– Sure. You sound a bit flat. What's happened?

– You remember Di?

I remember. It took him years to get over her when she left. This was long before he met Trish.

– Ran into her again, in the city. She's living down south now, nursing director of some hospital in Devon. She was in Manchester for a conference, she was in Finnegan's with a couple of girlfriends.

– How is she?

– I saw her, and I couldn't breathe. Twenty years, Mark.

– Oh, fuck.

– She's married now. So I let it be. That was last week.

Yesterday she rang me, says she can't stop thinking about me and wants to see me before she goes back to Exeter. I can't stop thinking about her either.

I call by his comfortable bungalow at the end of the village. There is a tree with blinking lights in the front room, gift-wrapped parcels underneath. Bah humbug. We drive to the local park. Greg can't sit still. He throws a rock at a duck.

– Did you ever feel this way about Trish? I ask him.

He shakes his head.

– Well. You know. I felt comfortable very early on in the piece.

– You never felt like this?

– Shit no.

He looks like a man who has run from a train wreck. I like him better like this, no longer sure of what is and what isn't. He is human, one of us after all.

– What are you going to do?

– I don't know. I don't know. I don't know.

Jesus. Life is giving him a second chance and he's hesitating.

It seems to me that I have fought this one all my life, fighting with Susan, then Anna, now Greg, wanting to shout at them, listen to your heart not your head! Don't compromise with life! Take a risk!

But this is not my call. Besides, isn't this what I did, hesitated on the edge until Susan changed the locks?

I give him the counsel I wish someone had given me: that this has to be about what he wants.

– First of all, make up your mind about you and Trish.

Forget about Dianne. Is what you have going to be enough?

– I don't know, Mark.

I shrug. If I've learned anything these last two years, it's that I don't have all the fucking answers.

– It's going to hurt Trish, he says.

– So your job is to protect other people from getting hurt?

– I care about her, Mark.

– I cared about Sue. But thinking I had to protect her turned me into the world's biggest liar. I kept telling her lies while I longed for someone else. Keeping her in the dark turned me into a prick of the first order.

He takes out a cigarette and lights it, thoughtfully. His hands are shaking.

– And there's Jay, he says, mentioning his son, who is now nineteen.

– Greg, I can't tell you what to do.

– Look at you and David. He's not forgiven you.

– Maybe he will, maybe he won't. But it's my life, not his. I'm his father but he can't tell me how to live.

A drift of light rain. We sit there.

– I don't know, he says again.

His cigarette burns to ash as he stares at the sky.

– Any regrets, Mark?

– You're nearly forty-five, Greg. You don't have time enough to listen to all my fuck-ups.

– Jeez, Mark. I've never felt anything like this. She walks in the room and I can't breathe.

I jump to my feet. This is too much. This is how I feel about Anna. I thought I was too sentimental, now I am hearing these same things from the most pragmatic and cautious man I know.

– This is not supposed to happen to me now, he says. I had everything settled in my life. This is going to throw everything out.

– How much of your life are you prepared to give up because you're too scared to take a risk?

– You think that's what it is? That I'm just scared?

– Yes.

That was blunt. He chews on it for a while. I'm one to lecture. I held on to Sue for as long as I could, simply out of fear.

– You think you can change your life and change how you feel without changing anything in it?

– I guess not.

– No, I say, mocking his indecision, I guess not.

He is quiet for a while.

– Can you love two women at once? he says suddenly, and hearing the words from him, when I have heard them so recently from Anna, is startling, like a jolt from a live wire.

– Of course. I still love Sue. But that's not the point.

He looks surprised at that, as if he thinks I stopped.

– I'll always love her. If love is caring deeply about someone, you can love lots of people at once, not just two. But this is about being in love, being in a relationship, living with someone. Are you getting what you need from Trish, are you giving her what she needs?

He thinks about this.

– I guess every man has his price, he says, and he means

Mark D'Arbanille

Dianne is his price, the one woman he might give up his ordered and secure life for. Perhaps.

– You're not going to reason your way out of this.

– So what's the answer?

– I don't know. Maybe you can ask yourself the question I asked myself when I was in your shoes.

– What was that?

– Do I want to be alive or feel alive?

He lights another cigarette. There is a look in his eyes, fear and calculation, how much he has to lose. It is probably safer and easier to do nothing, keep things as they are. I want to strangle him. His best chance, his golden chance to find the best in himself, and he is going to let it slip.

We all fear pain and change, yet it seems to me they are the only way we have of finding something better in our lives, and in ourselves. But what the hell do I know? This is not my life. Maybe I'm wrong. It wouldn't be the first time.

I stalk off across the park. A bright spring day and I want to kick someone's dog. So much love goes to waste, you'd think there was enough of it in the world to go round.

Ninety

Christmas Day I take David to a restaurant for Christmas lunch. I look around the room, recognise other families missing a father or mother, disoriented and exposed by the misery of holiday expectations.

The Christmas decorations and carols playing on the restaurant's sound system reinforce the hypocrisy of the mood. They might as well hang decapitated heads around the walls, for God's sake.

– This is a farce, David says.

I agree with him. What is there to say? I will not stay home and eat Christmas lunch in that echoing house so we have come here to be with other disjointed or troubled families. What does he want me to say?

– This is your fault.

I agree with him again. This is my fault, or at least, I was the one who instigated this turn of our family history.

He is sullen and silent. His anger diffuses into the air like

Mark D'Arbanville

gas. What can I say to him? He has lost his mother, and he feels his father has let him down. He is adrift, and in grief, and he needs a head to kick, and mine is right there. If I was his age I'd do the same thing.

I know I should just let this be. But my own pain takes over and I hear myself say, I'm sorry about what happened. But I couldn't stay with your mum just for you. That wasn't my job.

A lot of people would disagree. A lot of men and women do stay with someone they no longer love because of the children. There was an expectation upon me to do the same.

– She wouldn't have done this to you.

– No, she wouldn't.

You see, I want to shout at him, I agree with everything you think and say. What do you want me to do about this? I am more than a father and a husband! They were the roles I assumed but behind all this, look, here I am!

It doesn't mean I don't love you.

– What did you say? he asks.

I realise I have just spoken these simple words aloud.

– I said, it doesn't mean I don't love you.

He is silent. His eyes fill up. He is about to cry. I have not seen him cry since he was a small child. He brushes away a tear roughly with the back of his fist.

– I hate you, he says, but I know what he really means, and then the turkey dinner arrives and the stuffing is quite good and the potatoes are overdone and that is how we spend our second Christmas together without Sue.

Ninety-one

We stand for the women as they enter, there is fussing over wet coats and umbrellas and during the introductions, the shock of recognition. I have been invited to make up numbers at a dinner party in a Chinese restaurant. One of the men brings a woman he met at a party the week before, their first date. As she sits, our eyes lock in.

– I know you from somewhere, I say.

– Yes, you do, she answers, and she has the advantage of me.

Siobhan Leary. We had gone out for a while, I had ended the relationship when I met Susan.

There are many years to catch up on. We talk endlessly, and her new boyfriend gets tired of it and makes some excuse to leave. When the party breaks up Siobhan and I head for the coffee house next door, where I ask her why she never married.

A smile of embarrassment and pain.

– Oh, come on, what's the mystery?

A deep breath.

Mark D'Arbanville

– I was going out with a married man for seventeen years, she says.

I stare at her. Seventeen years. How can you keep up an affair for seventeen years? But then I had never imagined that my affair with Anna would last this long. Time slips past so fast.

I can't do this on your timetable.

– What happened?

– I loved him, she says simply, and I understand that, understand everything from these three words.

– I thought Tony would leave her. He kept hinting he would. And I loved him very much.

The red and blue lights on the coffee strip are reflected in the wet road. There is a draught of cold air as people arrive and leave, the hiss of tyres in the wet street very loud for a moment before the door closes again on the chatter and the steamy heat.

– You know how it is, she says, we'd split up, then we'd get back together again, then I'd leave him to work things out and he said he would but then I couldn't bear to be away from him and I'd go back.

A long silence.

– I don't know where the time went.

I suppose that is what time does, disappears while we are making up our minds what we are going to do with our lives.

– Last Christmas he bought me an outdoor setting. Do you know what he bought her?

I shake my head.

– A Merc.

I look up at the ceiling.

— Was it a very expensive outdoor setting? I ask her. It is a feeble attempt to ease the tension. It is the wrong thing to say. Her eyes fill up.

— What happened in the end?

— His wife found someone else. As soon as the kids were off her hands. All those years she kept saying she needed him and how could he do it to her, but as soon as she found someone else she packed and left almost overnight. Revenge, I suppose. Or she was just a selfish cow. Who knows?

She reaches for her bag, and tissues.

— I'm sorry.

My coffee is getting cold. I stir it endlessly with the spoon.

— So you finally got together?

— I got him by default, that was the trouble. His kids hated me and whenever they came round, he'd say, Siobhan, would you mind going out for a while, Alex is coming and he doesn't like it when you're here. He wouldn't stand up for me against them.

A terrible silence. I feel as if someone has kicked me in the stomach.

— Do you still see him? I ask her.

— I try not to. She leans towards me and whispers: *I thought if I just outlasted her, it would work out.*

She blows her nose into the tissue, and now she is embarrassed.

— You know what else I think? Never go out with a married man.

Hard not to be poisoned by hurt.

Mark D'Arbanville

We finish our coffees. I call her a cab and we shake hands in the rain.

Once I wondered what she was like in bed. Now I watch her get in the taxi and drive away.

Seventeen years.

Jesus.

Ninety-two

I think I will not see Siobhan again, but of course I do. I ring her up, just to talk, and she mentions the name of a French art house movie she wants to see, but none of her friends like films with subtitles and she doesn't like to go on her own and I tell her I am interested in the same movie and so we end up going to see it together. Then a few nights later we go out to dinner, and I drive her home and she asks me in for coffee. As I am leaving I hesitate for a moment at the door and she takes my face in her hands and kisses me.

I am not expecting this. I think about pulling away. But tonight Anna is sleeping with another man and perhaps I want to make a point, if only to myself. Or perhaps I am just lonely. It is not as if I feel nothing for her.

She is not Anna. But tonight I will pretend she is.

Mark D'Arbanville

Ninety-three

– So what are you going to do? Jen asks me.

The conundrum is this: I am unhappy and Anna thinks I cannot live without her. I become another weight on her back and she worries about hurting me more so she pushes me away.

If I move on, she will go back to her old life relieved that she is now square with the house, her sense of guilt and shame satisfied. She will console herself with the thought that everyone else is happy, although I imagine Anna will be left with the same problem: she is not.

And what about me? I cannot be with her, but if I leave I know there is a part of her that still wants me. She will not take away all hope or give me any. And this is not how she wants her life to be, so I know that sooner or later this must change.

Perhaps.

– Are you seeing someone else? Jen asks.

I shrug my shoulders.

— You've got to move on, she says. She won't ever leave him. She's stuck there. I bet she feels powerful and important being needed, being indispensable to a man she once worshipped. Once she lets go, she's out of control again.

— That's not true. You can't colour everything your way.

— Look, her whole life's been about taking care of other people. She'll feel too guilty to stop now. She's a people pleaser, Mark. She can't do anything for herself because she doesn't want anyone to hate her.

I wonder if Jen is talking about Anna or herself now. And I hate Jen describing Anna as a people pleaser, though this is how Anna once described herself.

— Anyway, men never leave. Not unless they have someone to go to. Everyone knows that, Mark. If she wants it to end, she'll have to move out herself or throw him out, and she's not strong enough to do that.

She's right about that: men never leave until they have something else to go to.

— If you stay in love with her, how will you ever let anyone else in?

— How do you forget the love of your life when she says she still loves you?

— You have to look after yourself.

— You mean compromise?

— We all do it, she says, and now she is talking about her and Terry. I know what she means. She will not let him go because there may not be someone better waiting for her, may not be anyone at all.

Mark D'Arbanville

So what will I do? Will I compromise with life, as Anna suggested, find another relationship, even though there is not this same inexplicable and breathless attraction? Anna has raised the bar too high.

I was not looking for anyone when I met her, she was the cliff I fell down while I was running towards my perfect picture. But what if love does come along a second time and I have compromised, as Jen is urging me to do? I will be back in exactly the same position I was in when I met Anna.

In other words, what kind of hopeless bastard am I really?

Ninety-four

A gloomy blue sky, the air redolent of spring and funeral ashes. A cool breeze carries with it the smell of dump fires. A man power-walking in a thick rollneck jumper and cheery scarf smiles and says *nice day* and I want to tell him to fuck off.

I walked with her hip to hip through this park. Today there are warmly dressed children laughing in the playground, lovers sitting entwined on benches, a beautiful day for the worst day of my life.

Her number is on my speed dial. I must remember to erase it.

I call her.

– I can't do this anymore, Anna. It's time to finish.

There is silence on the other end of the line.

– You're right, she says finally. It's not you, it's me. You deserve a hundred per cent. You deserve someone who can make you happy. And I can't give you that.

I knew that this is what she would say. It is no consolation.

Mark D'Arbanville

I don't expect ever to feel like this again. But what else is there to do?

— I don't think I'll ever get over this.

A man is throwing a stick for his dog. I hate him, hate this happiness everywhere, what's the point?

— I'm sorry for everything, she says.

— You said you loved me once.

— Perhaps I don't love you enough.

She is angry with me for ending it. It is in her voice, first the self recrimination *I'm sorry for everything* but that is the forerunner for her anger, because she wants, perhaps even needs, this to go on.

— I'll let you go now, I say, and end the call. Erase her numbers and all the stored messages. Walk back to the car. Drive home.

Better than an affair for seventeen years. Better than the outdoor furniture instead of the car.

I feel as if I am going to choke up my heart.

Ninety-five

I never imagined I could be this way.

I cannot work or sleep or eat. Small talk leaves me staring aimlessly into space. I fall asleep watching black and white foreign films at three in the morning. Bills lie around unpaid.

I pass a woman in the street wearing Lancôme Trésor and I turn and stare at her, I am about to say something to her, and she looks at me as if I am a stalker.

I put on a shirt and smell her scent on it, it is a shirt she once borrowed to wear to bed. Suddenly I cannot breathe. I have to sit down, overwhelmed with the enormity of my loss.

I call her and hang up before she can pick up the phone.

I arrange coffee with friends and then leave before my latte is even cold so I can be alone.

I wait for her to call but know she won't, she doesn't want to hurt me any more and even if she does want to call, it has

Mark D'Arbanville

always seemed that denying her own deeper desires is what she does best. For my sake, and for his.

I prowl the house like a wraith, a ghost bound to life and restless, unable to move on.

Ninety-six

I rent a small cabin on the Irish coast where I sometimes escaped with Anna. Her goodbye letter is forwarded on from Hanford.

I read it on the waterfront looking over the grey and churning sea and afterwards I scream back at the gulls as they wheel and screech on the wind. I cannot believe what she has written.

I do love you with all my heart and soul . . . .

If this is true, then what part of her heart and soul is there left for Paul? This cannot be true. Or perhaps it is the heart and soul of the Anna that I love; there must be a different heart and soul for Paul.

. . . at times I have been the other life, the refuge
from pain in your life as well, I know not in the
same way as I have done it . . .

. . . you are the most incredibly talented,
romantic, caring and giving man I have ever met.
Your love moves me to the very core of my soul.
I wanted you as my secret, something no one else
would touch. I did not expect to fall in love with you
or you with me . . .

If we need a refuge from our lives, I shout at the fishing boats drifting in the harbour, what does that tell us about our husbands and wives?

You are a beautiful wonderful man who has touched
my soul and continues to do so every day. Your writing
is lyrical, your laugh and mind magical, I think about
you every day . . .

I do not understand what is happening here. I am utterly bewildered. If this letter is true, what does this leave for Paul? He must know she is elsewhere. How can he settle for this?

This is not how she wants her life to be. She does not want her life tormented by loving two men. She has one foot on the ferry and the other on the quay, and the boat is leaving the dock. And yet she hesitates.

What about me? How do I love again, clear my heart of her when I know the same wonderful woman I have loved above any other feels this way about me still? Yet the last time I spoke to her she told me that she did not love me enough.

I am lost, blinded, tripping in a hall of mirrors. How do

you stop loving the love of your life when she says she still loves you?

Before today, I had convinced myself she had simply changed her mind, that my anger and constant carping had eroded the love she once had for me. But with this letter I feel my soul unravelling piece by piece, like someone pulling at the threads of a jumper.

For two months the letter haunts me. And then one night I get a call from her friend Sally telling me that Anna has been in an accident and may not make it through the night.

I get in the car and drive to London.

Mark D'Arbanille

Ninety-seven

It is the moment I have dreaded, the one moment that she said she could never forgive, the moment I make myself real.

Susan is sitting on the edge of the bed, unseen by the others. She is holding Anna's hand; these two women are reaching to each other on either side of the mortal borderlands.

As a very little child I made the decision for whatever reason to fit in, to feel special, to be approved of, to be needed and because I felt rewarded for being like that I lived out my life this way.

Did this dutiful wife and daughter lurch in front of that removalist's van by accident or did her foot stray from the brake deliberately?

The family are all watching me. These are people I know from Anna second hand, and now they are flesh and blood.

I look around the room. Paul is just as I imagined him. Her father, Derek, looks utterly bewildered. Her sisters and her mother are huddled together. I suspect they know who I am.

I could expose her easily now, and I always thought this was what I wanted. But this is not about me or Paul. If she does not confront this dilemma herself, there is no healing, for her or for me.

She has perhaps concealed her pain from her family, as I suspect she has always done. But whether she tells them or not, and who she decides to be with, this is not my crusade. She must make the decision alone, as I did, as Sue did.

But where is me in all this and who is me?

It has been better to be busy and keep busy than uncover this truth.

Of late I have desperately tried to cling on to the people in my life who have defined who I am rather than face the frightening prospect of having to define me for myself.

If I gave my husband the power to make decisions about who or what I am then the implicit agreement is that he'll look after me and I won't be alone ever.

I have to trust and listen to the voice inside.
I know I'll continue to die inside and begin to die outside if I don't do this.

They are all staring at me, wondering what I will say.

– This is Mark, Sally says, suddenly appearing at my side. He's a friend of mine.

Mark D'Arbanville

She puts a proprietary arm through mine. A clever girl, Sally. She had this planned, of course, knew how it would look.

— What's he doing here? Anna's father says.

— He knew Anna. He was . . . fond of her.

I see it in their eyes. They all know who I am now, except her father, but nobody wants to break this bond of silence.

Sally steers me out of the room and says she will meet me in the cafeteria. When she comes down she is grave.

— The doctors have told them she's out of danger, but they don't know how much damage there is. She may not wake up. If she does wake, they don't know how she'll be. She may not remember anything.

Anna without a past. An interesting concept and even now I have to smile at such a thought. What will Anna do, how will she live her life if there is nothing to remember of the past? Anna with a clean slate. What will she make of Paul? Of her family? Or of me?

But she will not remember me, because I will not be here to remind her. Perhaps I will meet her again, at some film conference somewhere, and she will see me, once again, for the very first time. What will happen then?

— Are you all right? Sally asks.

I shake my head, but do not trust myself to speak. Finally:

— Thanks for letting me know, Sally.

— You can't tell them who you really are, she says.

I nod, I understand this. I am still her secret. The Anna that loves me is still a secret from them.

I pick up my coffee cup but my hands are shaking so badly

I spill the coffee on the laminated top and I clunk the cup back into its saucer.

– Did you see what happened?

– I was in the car behind her.

– Was it deliberate?

She shrugs. The only one who knows has the answer locked inside her head, as she always has.

I feel numb. This is too much grief to cope with. I have loved this woman as I have never loved anyone.

– How are you, Sally?

Her bottom lip quivers.

– I don't understand this. She's lovely. Why can't she be happy?

– She has secrets, I say.

– I wish she'd let them out. Can anything be that bad?

– I always had the feeling that we wouldn't think so, but that she did.

Later, when we go back to the ICU, the family are not there, are talking in another room with her surgeon. A nurse is standing at the foot of Anna's bed, making notes on her chart.

God, don't let her die. Even if I never see her again, don't let her die.

– I'll give you some time alone, Sally whispers to me, and leaves.

After the nurse has gone, I sit down next to the bed and pick up her hand in both of mine, as she once did in that London hotel so many lifetimes ago.

– Hey, babe, I whisper. Christ. What a mess. Look, they

252

Mark D'Arbanville

say you won't remember anything when you wake up. They'll have to tell you what your life is. They'll tell you who you're married to, who your family are, even what you want and what you do.

I run a finger along the back of this small, pale hand. I kiss her fingers.

– But you have to remember, Anna. You have to remember everything. What you forget will always torment you, it will hide away in there and you won't even know what it is that's troubling you.

I will survive without her. But it will be just that, going through days without the meaning and colour she brought. Life in monochrome. Some people know the feeling, this love at first sight. I don't know whether to think them lucky or unfortunate.

– Goodbye, honey.

I look up. Paul is standing in the doorway. I wonder how much he has heard. I release her hand. For a moment we stare at each other.

I get to my feet. One hand hangs limp at his side. The other opens and closes in a fist.

I wonder what to say to him. He nods his head and smiles, is about to let me pass without a word. He will pretend I am Sally's friend. If he speaks, I might become real.

– You know who I really am, Paul.

He shakes his head, undecided what to do about this.

– I love her, he says.

And he does, of course. But the Anna he loves is perhaps not the real Anna, as the man Susan loved was never really me.

– For a long time, I wanted to kill you, he says.

– Why didn't you ever talk about me with her?

He doesn't answer.

I guess the answer aloud:

– Because if you talked to her about me, you might find out she really wasn't the woman you thought she was. Neither of you wanted that. Not you, and not Anna.

– You shouldn't have come here.

I am surprised to find that I neither hate him nor envy him. Once I thought he was lucky. If he loses her, I know what it will be like for him, for I have lost her many times now, and the aggregation of grief has hollowed me out inside. But even if he keeps her, he does not want the part of her that she has shown me, he wants her as she was in the past. And so he does not even love the very part of her that I adore. He is not lucky at all, for I suspect he has missed the very best of her, it's not what he needs.

– What are you going to do? he asks me.

– I planned on going home.

– She'll never leave.

– That's what all my friends say, too.

I hesitate at the door.

– I'm sorry, Paul. I didn't mean to hurt you like this. I know you love her. But if it wasn't me, something else would have happened to tear things up between you. She's not who you think she is. There's more in her heart than you know.

The alarm sounds on Anna's ECG. Nurses and a resident run into the room and reset the machine and prepare to resuscitate her. Paul and I watch, stricken, from just inside the

Mark D'Arbanville

doorway. But it is a false alarm. Whatever disturbed her monitor was phantom. The arrhythmia corrects itself.

Anna's mother is waiting in the corridor outside, with Anna's sisters. All I can do now is walk away. They will think they imagined me; or rather, that Anna did, and I suppose that really was what happened.

We all tell ourselves we will live for ever and that we have so much time; but we have no time at all, none to waste. Death is there to keep us honest, even if we are not. God allows all of us just enough time for fulfilment, for change, or to die undecided, as we so choose.

And now Anna is looking into death's dark face also. Perhaps in her opiate dreams she stares down the same stark choices that Sue faced.

I am dying because the way I have lived for the last forty years is not working any more. I did this but at the price of never being there for myself, or at the cost of being so busy with everything else that I never had time for me. I have desperately tried to cling to the external people in my life who have defined who I am than face the frightening prospect of having to define me for myself. My work has defined me and without it I don't know who I'd be any more.

What will Anna do?

Will she wake invigorated from her brush with mortality, refreshed by forgetfulness? Will she then be free to fly, fly wherever she wishes?

Or will she wake and smile in instant recognition at these worried parents and siblings and husbands and accept back the life she had before?

Or will she stay asleep, here in this hospital bed, months to years, numb from it all?

Only another woman will know the answer to this; and if you are a woman you know already what Anna will do, she will do as you would do, as you do already, every day of your living life.

Mark D'Arbanille

Ninety-eight

— **So what are you** going to do, Mark? Who are you going to fuck next?

Jen is drunk, talking too much and too loudly and the other drinkers in the snug are staring and she doesn't give a shit. It's what I love and dread about her.

— Do you mean that in the Biblical sense or in the sense of disturbing someone's emotional and intellectual stability?

She waves the hand that has the wine glass in it and wooded chardonnay glops onto the oak table.

— Oh well, you know. Whatever.

— I don't know what I'm going to do.

— You always attract troubled women, don't you? What is it with that?

— If I knew, I'd probably try and stop it happening.

— Look at you. They must love you. The safe, nice guy who won't dump them, or hurt them, but also a bit of a wild guy who'll show them a good time before he reaches his use-by date. That's the story of your life, isn't it?

Jen is right. All my relationships have followed the same pattern, before and after Sue. I have always looked for a good woman and a wild woman in the same package but I never really found her until Anna. Most women I have known have either been safe or wild. I hate the wild women because they leave me and I hate the safe women because they are too safe.

Jen is drunk and slurring her words.

— Trouble with you, you think everything is black and white. And it's not. You're both fucked up, Mark. You're both trying to live with two people.

— I'm not. Sue's not here anymore, remember?

— I don't mean Sue and Peter —

— Paul.

— Whatever. I mean the two people that live inside you. You're both schizophrenic, you and this Anna. That's the attraction between you, isn't it?

— Speak up a bit, Jen. They can't quite hear you in Reykjavik.

— You still miss Sue, don't you? And there's a bit of Sue in Anna, isn't there, and you won't admit it.

— Yes, okay, there's some Sue in Anna. But there's something else, and that's what I've been looking for.

She laughs and slams her drink down, more white wine all over the polished oak table and she doesn't pay any attention.

— You see! That's what I tried to tell you, you bastard!

What I wanted was to love and laugh again. We couldn't do that together any more. It didn't make my wife a bad woman. Did it make me a terrible man?

Mark D'Arbanille

– I was a different man when I met Sue. I'd never lived with a woman before, I wanted someone to hold at night, a good friend.

– A safe house where you could build your career.

No. Yes. Maybe. Sue was enough then. It was only when I looked around at my life a few years later, when work and the bank book and the car and the house were all sorted, that I wondered if there was more.

– I thought the problem was me. That I wanted too much. I hated myself for it. I thought if I ignored this bastard in my head, he'd go away.

– Why didn't you do something about it earlier? Like before you got married?

– He only turned up in my thirties, when the rest of my life was sorted. Until then he was just this sort of vague . . . itch. But suddenly it was like Jekyll and Hyde. No matter how hard I tried to keep the bastard out of my life, I couldn't stay away from him. He kept taking over more and more, this reckless shit up against the good family man. I thought, well, only one of these guys can win out. I hated that other bastard, I was ashamed of him. But he was also the part of me that made me feel alive. I knew he wanted more than Sue could ever give.

– Then you met Anna.

– And she fell for Mr Hyde.

– That's why you wanted to keep both women in your life! Jen announces to the whole pub, alcohol assuming complete control of her vocal cords.

That's why you wanted to keep both women in your life!

I remember the email I sent Anna, all those centuries ago, after she first left me. It sounded so perfect; I would have a wife and a mistress, she would have a husband and a secret lover. Neither of us would disrupt our family lives and I could continue this unique friendship for ever and no one would get hurt. She would satisfy Mr Hyde and I would be salve for her demons also.

– It could never work, Jen says.

I think we blew it away, Jen. Sue and I lost sight of what it was. I wanted a free spirit that I could keep on a leash. She resented my control but leaned on me anyway. We were a perfect match. But that's not how it started. I don't know how it got to be that way. Perhaps she thought when she became a wife and a mother things had to be different but she was still a woman, and it was the woman I starved out. And so did she. I don't know, maybe it's the same story for Anna and Paul. You can't win.

But it was my call. No reason to feel sorry for myself.

– And what about you and Terry? I ask her. Does he love both the women in you?

– There's only one of me these days. Can I have another drink?

– You really think you should?

– Yeah, Jen shouts in my face. I want to get pissed!

She empties her glass.

– It's late, Jen. I mean, I don't mind, but won't Terry be wondering where you are?

– He won't be home yet, she says. And then she starts to cry.

Mark D'Arbanville

Christ. I put a hand on her shoulder to comfort her and she collapses into my chest and starts to sob. I feel wetness on my shirt.

– My life is a fucking mess, Jen says.

Life is about compromise, of course, but you have to know what is compromise and what is selling out.

Ninety-nine

Siobhan sits naked on the edge of the bed. I admire her silhouette in the yellow light of the bedside lamp, long-backed, sleek and blonde. She is utterly gorgeous and more available than Anna and much, much easier. So why don't I forget about Anna?

A voice inside my head tells me that's the smart thing but there's another voice that says if I do, I will be betraying a big part of myself.

She lights a joint and passes it to me.

– Tell me about Anna, Siobhan says.

I experience a minor panic attack when any girlfriend asks me about her. How do they know to work the scab off this particular wound? Is it because women have such wonderful intuition or because I am so transparent?

– What do you want to know?

– What was she like?

How do you answer a question like that? I don't really know what she was like, I saw the part of her I was allowed to

Mark D'Arbanville

see, apparently a part of her that no one else saw, or so she said. So what was she like? I can only hazard a guess.

– She was like me.

She frowns, puzzled.

– She was two people in one. She was crazy. She was confused. She was lost. And she was pretending.

Siobhan laughs. She's not sure if I'm teasing her, and I've made her nervous. I am here tonight, in her bed, because she thinks I am what I seem to be, safe and honest and charming and gentle with a quirky sense of humour. Not because I am crazy and lost.

– That's not you, she says.

Of course, Anna would not say that if she were here. Anna would laugh and say, yes, we're both crazy, Mister D'Arbanville. Anna knows this other side of me as well as she knows the crazy part of herself, and that is perhaps why she waited up for me until four in the morning that night two years ago; not for an affair or an adventure, but because she recognised a kindred spirit.

– If Anna ever left her husband, what would you do? Siobhan asks me.

Christ. I have never thought about this question since I started sleeping with Siobhan. I should be able to answer this straight away, but instead I let the silence drag and it seems forever before I finally assure her that it would make no difference to me.

As reward, Siobhan kisses me on the mouth. She tastes of grass and white wine and smells of Gaultier and sex. She looks like a goddess. What is wrong with me?

What is wrong is that there is no edge to her. She likes

what I write and create, but she doesn't love it passionately, as Anna does. We connect, of course, but Anna understands we are two people and Siobhan thinks I am what she sees.

Anna gets me.

Like Anna, like me, Siobhan seeks out the everyday allure of familiarity and a warm body at night. Without that edge I suspect I will one day die of boredom.

But Siobhan is here, and she is here tonight. As Paul is with Anna.

Siobhan takes my hand and holds it to her breast. She is so beautiful.

— Tell me you love me, she whispers.

— I love you, I tell her.

There. That wasn't so bad, was it?

Mark D'Arbanville

One hundred

– How's Anna? Greg asks.
   – I don't call, I don't ask.
   She must be on the road to recovery by now, I imagine. Has she forgotten everything? If she has, I'm history. An interesting expression, because in fact I won't be a part of anyone's history except my own.
   Paul and her father and her family know about me now. If she does remember, they will do everything to ensure she does not see me or call me. I am too real, the wayward husband with the dead wife and the errant son, how unsuitable could a man be? Not the kind of man to parade at family birthdays.
   – Will you be my best man?
   – Honoured, Greg.
   Greg and Di have made it, if getting married is the same as making it. There is a sense of satisfaction for me here.
   Greg is disgustingly happy at an age when we are supposed

to be resigned. Will this last? I have great hopes for them, for destiny led Greg back to the one woman he always loved, and he and Dianne worked it out this time around. I feel a sense of triumph. Sometimes things do pan out.

Greg orders another round of beers.

– To be honest, I never thought you'd take the risk.

– You just have to know what your bottom line is, he says, my pupil now my mentor. You have to ask yourself: what is it I won't compromise on?

– I don't know.

He taps his forehead with a finger.

– She fits me, Mark. I mean, not knows me, because Trish knew me, knew everything I've done the last fifteen years. But Di fits me.

His eyes are shining. A passion in him I have not seen before.

– It's not perfect, Mark. Nothing ever is, I suppose. Her family don't like me, but maybe that will change, give it time. Don't know if Jay will ever take to her, either, Christmases will be awkward for a few years. It's not the perfect picture I had once.

– You amaze me.

He shrugs:

– What can I say? Sometimes it works out, sometimes it doesn't. Fate, I suppose.

– I don't believe in fate.

This is what I believe: that fate is meeting the perfect woman at a writers conference. After that it's up to you what happens.

Mark D'Arbanville

– Just don't compromise on the things that really matter, Mark. The things that get you here. He taps his chest.

Greg, the romantic. How the wheel turns. Funny, I now believe that I myself will err on the side of caution. What has happened to Anna has dispirited me. After so long I suspect I am not strong enough to go down with the ship.

One hundred and one

And so I have moved on.

I miss her tonight, as the rain leaks down the window and tree branches scrape the metal roof of the beach cabin.

I surf through my laptop folders, picking emails that I sent her at random. I cannot believe my own arrogance, the superior tone of them, how I once tried to tell her what to do and what to think, like every other man in her life.

I remember when I had my life under control, all those centuries ago, and yet just three years, that dark age in my history when I gauged everything by what I had and what others thought of me. I loved how they said how perfect my life was, and yet I hated it also, there was always that small voice that reminded me: *but you're not happy.*

I walk along the cliffs, take out the cigar box she sent me one birthday. *To my lover and my best friend.* I rub the engraving with my fingers, draw in the smoke and watch the sea batter the rocks below.

Mark D'Arbanville

We stayed here together once, in those days when I thought she might change her mind. I cooked her curries and we made love on the floor as she dripped oil over her body and knelt over me so I could watch her breasts gleam in the light of a candle.

If Anna had not come into my life I would still be wrestling with that same restless yearning, feeling trapped, fighting with Susan, living out uneasy truces, dreading Valentine's Days and birthdays and the future as I had year after year for so long.

I do not believe anyone can ever be quite like this woman who came into my life by accident when I wasn't looking.

– Can I ask you a personal question? Are there, like, hundreds of men in your life or just one really lucky one?

Now I wonder how lucky he is, for I wonder if he ever saw the Anna I have known; her passion in bed, how she can talk for hours about life, and about people and about books. How she can lose herself in the world of ideas, and the imagination, how she can dance for hours and drink champagne and knock on your hotel room door at two in the morning pretending to be a Russian masseuse. These are not things Paul ever wanted from her and so we have loved and fought over different women.

Susan loved a different man also, not the man Anna adored. I am learning to accept them both, but how to find a companion for them yet eludes me.

There comes an age when we all must decide whether we

will fulfil that essential urging of the spirit or just live to survive. Perhaps save the lesson for next time.

Now I ask myself the same questions that Sue demanded of herself.

But where is me in all this and who is me?
It has been better to be busy and keep busy than uncover this truth. Of late I have desperately tried to cling on to the people in my life who have defined who I am rather than face the frightening prospect of having to define me for myself.

The alchemists of the Middle Ages searched for what they called the philosopher's stone, the curious object that could turn lead into gold by some alchemy never explained. Some men thought it was an actual substance, but for the mystics the stone was an allegory for something else, something that could change a man into something better.

Anna was my philosopher's stone; there was a chemistry that for all of her faults and all of mine made us both see love in colour, and turned my base metal into gold, at least when I was with her.

Sometimes we leave people we should never lose; sometimes we stay with others much too long.

The next day I get on a plane and fly back to Manchester. I have a wedding to go to. Why is it I feel a part of me is dying?

I am dying because the way I have lived for the last forty years is not working any more. I did this but at

Mark D'Arbanville

*the price of never being there for myself, or at the cost
of being so busy with everything else that I never had
time for me. I have desperately tried to cling to the
external people in my life who have defined who I
am than face the frightening prospect of having to
define me for myself. My work has defined me and
without it I don't know who I'd be any more. I have
to trust and listen to the voice inside. I know I'll
continue to die inside and begin to die outside if
I don't do this.*

*I wonder if I can do this. I wonder if I can trust.
I wonder if I can listen to that inner voice.*

And so to a Saturday afternoon in September. I stare out of
the window of the limousine and let my mind drift through
the blown leaves of these last three years and try to make some
sense of all that has happened. It is a jigsaw with many missing pieces, frustrating because I have worked so hard on this
enervating task, and there is nothing left to fit into the frame
yet it still appears not quite complete.

I turn a white card in my fingers, my thumb tracing
the contours of gold embossing: *You are invited to celebrate the
marriage of . . .*

The Mercedes stops outside the church. Greg raises his
eyebrows and smiles, taps me on the shoulder. We both get out
and walk around the side to the vestry door. I stop for one last
cigar, to steady the nerves, and a draught from the hip flask
Greg has in his pocket. The wind disturbs the leaves in the
oak in the graveyard. I take a deep breath and now, too late,

wish I had been a stronger man, or a luckier one. But I have decided that love will never give me what I want. I hoped for too much, and laid my heart too bare. It is time to smarten up.

> *. . . celebrate the marriage of Siobhan O'Leary and*
> *Mark D'Arbanville at St Mary's Anglican Church*
> *in . . .*

My cell phone rings, playing the Dance of the Valkyries. Must remember to turn it off now we're at the church. A tightening in my gut when I see the caller's name displayed on the screen: it's Sally.

— Hey, Sally.

— Mark, how are you doing?

It's a real enquiry, genuine concern here. What can I say? Three months since I last spoke to her, perhaps she hasn't heard.

— I'm okay.

The response is so vague, and so untrue, I want to laugh at myself.

— I thought you ought to know . . .

Oh God. My heart like a fist tightening in my chest.

— Anna's awake.

— Is she okay?

— She came out of it about a week ago. She wants to talk to you, Mark.

She wants to talk to you. The words echo around the church-yard, drowning out the din of crows in the beeches. I should hang up now. This is over, this is done.

Mark D'Arbanville

I take a deep breath. Greg's forehead knits into a frown.

– You okay?

I don't answer. I end the call without another word.

– What's up? Greg asks again. Mark?

Okay, so I am compromising here today. Selling myself short. Isn't that what everyone does sooner or later?

– You ready, mate?

– Give me a minute, I say, and walk off alone, stare at the gravestones in the churchyard. Look how many years people really have, even the old ones. It's not long, is it?

What would you do if you were me? Would you go back, knowing you have never felt this way about any woman before? Do you find out if there is such a thing as a miracle for a man like you?

Or do you accept that God does not want us to love too much, cut your losses and follow Greg inside the church?

I hesitate, staring at the cell phone. On moments such as this, whole lifetimes turn.